Reign of Wicked Temptation

JEN BRADLEE

REIGN OF WICKED TEMPTATION

Copyright © 2022 Kirsten S. Blacketer/Jen Bradlee.

This is a work of fiction. Similarities to real people, places, or events are entirely coincidental.

Printed in the United States of America.
First Printing, 2022
ISBN: 978-1966905165

Cover Art by The Midnight Muse
Written by Jen Bradlee
Published by BlackShip Press
Kirsten.blacketer@gmail.com
https://kirstensblacketer.com/jen-bradlee/

Dedication

We all deserve a happy ending. Even if we're irredeemable assholes.
Thanks for reading!

A Letter from the Author

Dear Reader,

Welcome and thank you for selecting *Reign of Wicked Temptation* for your reading pleasure. I truly hope you enjoy the story and fall in love with the characters.

Allow me to preface with a warning. If you're not a fan of anti-heroes with dominating and questionable morals, explicit intimate scenes, or graphic language and violence, then this may not be the book for you. For a complete list of content forewarnings, please visit kirstensblacketer.com/jen-bradlee.

If that's exactly what you're looking for, then allow me to welcome you and proceed. Thank you for choosing The Prince of Whispers as your literary companion.

Sending warm regards and best wishes your way. Remember to be kind and love one another.

Sincerely,

Jen Bradlee

Table of Contents

Year 1442 A.D.
SCOTLAND
IRELAND
ENGLAND
Northern Hold
Marian's Cottage
Balmont Holding
Monastery
Culver
MERADIN
WALES
KEY
Capital
Landmark
Village
Port

Chapter One

A scream pierced the darkness. Henry gasped and coughed, a familiar metallic taste burning his tongue. He groaned and pressed his hands against the cold stone floor. His body ached worse than it ever had after sparring or a long day in the saddle. Worse than when he and Crispin took down a band of thieves on the border, and he earned himself a scar on his side as payment for his good deed. The pain hung heavy around his shoulders, pinning him to the floor. The abrasive stone cooled his cheek. Even as he struggled to right himself, his limbs refused to cooperate.

Henry took several deep breaths and rested, willing his body to function. Where was he? Flashes of the altercation in the forest flickered in the back of his mind. Riding along the moonlit road. The wagon blocking their path. The raiders.

"Ruby!" Henry shouted with the effort it took to push himself up. Where was she? Had they taken her? Killed her? Where was he? The questions trudged through his mind, slowed by the haze of pain radiating through him. His head pounded like a hammer against an anvil, and his limbs ached with heaviness, protesting with every movement. Whoever took them captive must have beat him while he was unconscious. Never before had he experienced such agony ripping him apart from the inside.

The room contained a bed along the wall and a pot in the corner. Try as he might, he could not focus on the items in the room. He blinked attempting to clear his vision. Henry touched his face, covering his swollen right eye. The blur cleared into solid forms. He made a conscious effort to keep his injured eye closed and surveyed the room once more.

A prison cell. The sliver of light came through a thin slat in the solid wooden door held in place with iron hinges. Gripping the edge of the bed, Henry pulled himself up but stumbled at the tightening pressure around his ankle. He jerked his feet, dragging a chain across the stone. Manacles bound his feet, fastened to the wall by a chain.

Fighting against the restrictive bonds, Henry managed to pull himself up and sit on the bed. Another scream pierced the silence. His heart pounded harder, sweat formed on his neck, sliding over his skin and sending a shiver down to his bones.

Henry leaned against the wall in an effort to regain his balance. Nausea overwhelmed him. Had he anything in his stomach, it would have spilled with little resistance. He braced himself as the waves slowly subsided. He pressed his eyes closed, fighting off the instability of his vision. It reminded him of the sea voyage to France where he spent most of the trip bent over the rails unable to stand or eat. This was no voyage. This was far worse than he could have ever imagined.

He licked his cracked lips, tasting the blood caked upon them. He moaned at the sting and longed for the sweet, refreshing kiss of a mountain spring or a dram of mead, anything to quench his thirst and clear his mind.

Another scream echoed from beyond the door and gripped his soul. *Ruby.*

Ignoring the protests of his body and the limits of his chains, Henry shot off the bed and lunged for the door. The manacles snapped tight, bringing him to an abrupt halt and slamming him down onto the ground. Jarred, Henry struggled to his feet, bracing his hand against the cold stone wall.

Murmured voices filtered through the narrow slat in the door. He could make out nothing but the low cadence of two distinct voices.

"Release me, you sniveling bastards!" Henry shouted. His voice broke mid-curse, hoarse from disuse and thirst.

"You live. What a pity. I had a wager you would die during the night." A deep chuckle filtered through the slat.

Henry glared with his good eye trying to glimpse his captor, but he saw nothing but a shadow against the wood. "Where is she?"

"The queen is no longer your concern." The man's tone implied his malicious intent toward both of his captives.

"If you harm her, I will eviscerate you and leave your rotting carcass for the crows," Henry growled. His hands balled into tight fists.

"You waste what little breath remains in you." Even though he could not see the man's expression, pleasure reflected in his words. "If you persist, I shall be forced to punish the queen for her guard's inability to follow direction."

Even though he never relayed Ruby's state, Henry took this information as a sign she was not dead as he feared. He inhaled deeply, allowing this small shred of hope to fill him with a steadying peace.

"Whatever game you play at, you will not win. The king will come for her." Henry chuckled at the horrifying image his words brought to mind. Crispin would certainly come, and he would show no mercy. "He will slaughter you with pleasure, as well as anyone who follows your direction."

"He is inept and consumed by childish, petty distractions." His captor sounded bored. "The queen and the kingdom are no longer his. History will regard him as nothing more than a stain on the royal bloodlines of Europe."

"The people of Meradin are loyal to King Crispin and Queen Eleanor." Strength infused Henry. "This act of treason will not stand."

Coarse laughter met his statement. "Once the people see the man beneath the crown for what he truly is, a selfish, deceitful imposter hellbent on his own personal gratification at the expense of those around him, they will turn their hearts." The amusement faded. "Even after he used you for his own perverse pleasure, you stand steadfast in his service. Such loyalty is misplaced."

A chill coursed through Henry. "My loyalty is mine to do with as I see fit."

"And your body, does that also belong to you, or does your king control it as well?" The faceless villain tormented him.

Henry shook his head, reigniting the stabbing pain. "I know not what you imply with such venomous assumptions, but I am my own master."

"You went willingly to his chamber. Indulged in wicked acts with them both freely of your own will?" Hearing it aloud brought shame and uncertainty.

"You rely far too heavily on the whispers of servants and idle gossip." He swallowed the fear rising in the back of his throat. His chest tightened as the walls around him crept closer.

"The truth matters not. Rumors and gossip foster revolution. The people will demand a king who will not desecrate their kingdom for his own wicked desires." The captor tisked. "'Tis better if you concede defeat. No one is coming. Death will bring the relief you crave. Freedom is merely an illusion."

Before Henry could respond, the sound of receding footsteps echoed beyond the door.

"You son of a bitch! You will burn in hell for this, mark my words!" His throat burned from the effort he expended. He screamed and the anguish escaped, sliding off the stone and filling his soul with grief. How could he have allowed this to happen?

He should never have taken Ruby out of the castle. He endangered them all with his careless actions, and they now suffered the consequences of his poor decision. Ruby was alive, for the moment. That alone gave him comfort, and yet he knew that comfort would be short-lived. Whoever captured them had much larger plans than he first assumed.

Their captor intended to use the queen to force the king's hand. They would take the throne by force. Blood would fill the streets if he successfully turned the people against the monarchy. Those who were loyal to Crispin would suffer.

He could not focus on something out of his control. First and foremost, he needed a way to escape and steal Ruby away from this madman.

Henry rested his head against the wall. Who could possibly want to tear the kingdom apart? There were many who disliked Crispin and wished to remove him from the throne. But none he knew of were brazen enough to invoke his wrath by taking the queen.

Ignoring the pain and his thirst, Henry took what tools were given to him and replayed the events leading to their capture. If all he had was time, he would use it to the best advantage. There was always hope, even if it felt helpless. If only he could force himself to believe it long enough to survive.

Chapter Two

Bile bit the back of her throat. Ruby blinked against the darkness. Small pinpoints of light filtered through the fabric like the sky on a clear, cold night. Her head ached, and she struggled to breathe with the sack covering her face.

Ignoring the pounding in her head and the numbness in her bound limbs, she struggled against the bonds around her hands. Her feet twisted to no avail. The soft fabric beneath her belied the comforts of a bed and fine linens, but the scent was unfamiliar. It could be the fabric covering her head, but there was nothing comfortable about her situation in truth. She was a captive.

Flashes of images appeared in her mind as she recalled the altercation in the forest. The men who chased her. A long trek through the dark woods. The outline of the castle on the sunlit horizon. Hope and relief had filled her. She saw salvation.

Ruby remembered nothing after the blinding pain save the darkness. She fought against the bonds harder, grunting from the effort and willing the knots to loosen. Her breath came faster, making it more difficult to fill her lungs with air. The fabric of the sack stuck to her sweat-slickened cheek and tangled hair.

Inhaling deeply, she loosed a scream to bring down the walls of Jericho. If there be any hope, it would come. Or her captor would. Either way, Ruby could assess the situation more clearly if she knew where she was. And whom she had to thank for their generous hospitality.

Silence met her outburst. She opened her mouth to scream again, but the sound of a lock being turned made her pause and listen. The soft shuffle of footsteps entered the room. Ruby stilled as they came closer.

Whoever entered the room placed something on a hard

surface. A tray perhaps. Or a weapon. It was difficult to tell. She strained to hear anything that might give her an idea of where she was.

"Who are you?" Ruby's voice cracked on the final word, but she held firm awaiting the intruder's response.

The faint scent of roasted meat and apples teased her hunger to life. Her stomach growled, and her mouth watered. She swallowed and pushed aside the temptation.

"What do you want?" Ruby demanded with a stronger determination.

A soft brush of fingertips against the back of her hand made Ruby recoil. "Show yourself. Coward." She struggled again, knowing it was hopeless but the thought of someone placing their hands upon her without consent incensed her. "Release me!"

The room filled with the sound of soft feminine laughter followed by the retreat of footsteps and the slamming of the door. Ruby swore and writhed on the bed. Her frustration boiled over into pure panic. She screamed again louder than before. Whoever dared to accost her would pay dearly.

After fighting her unbreakable binding, she lay still with her heart pounding and breath heaving. How she longed for the cool air against her skin. Her nose itched, making her eyes water. Curse this bastard.

Her stomach growled again seduced by the meal brought by some faceless woman. Instead of focusing on the food, she directed her thoughts to assess her situation.

How much time had passed? Hours. Days. It was impossible to tell. Crispin would surely know of her disappearance by now. But how would he know where she was taken or by whom? The bandits set upon them with the intent to take her, but they would show no mercy to her escorts. Henry and Connor were surely dead. A third scream wrenched itself from her throat filled with agony and pain.

Unrelenting guilt consumed her. She caused their deaths as surely as she had drawn a blade from her own sheath and drove it into their hearts. Tears filled her eyes. Nay. She blinked them away. There had to be hope. Perhaps they escaped as she did. Even if one of them returned to the castle and raised the alarm, it would be better than imagining them both dead along the king's road.

Ruby pinched her eyes closed and took several calming breaths. She wiggled her fingers, flexing life back into them where the cool prickling sensations tingled beneath her skin. Willing herself to focus on anything but the hopelessness of her situation, Ruby whispered a prayer.

Crispin would come. He vowed he would always find her. She prayed harder.

The suspended silence of her thoughts shattered at the sound of an animal howling in pain. Her heart constricted. That was not the sound of an animal in agony—'twas a man. The lonely, piercing cry of a captive echoed through the walls of stone. The realization led her from sympathy to hope. Perhaps one of her knights had been spared.

Ruby licked her lips. A hundred thoughts raced through her mind, but with the restrictions hampering her, she could do no more than lie in wait for an opportunity.

This time she heard the solid footsteps approach the door. Her ears pricked at the sound of the lock turning and the sturdy creak of the hinges when the door opened. She stiffened at the shift in the air.

Ruby held her breath as the footsteps grew louder until they ceased completely. She squealed with surprise as she was hauled up into a sitting position on the edge of the bed. A firm pair of hands steadied her when she swayed at the sudden motion. She wrenched herself away from the unwelcome touch.

"Get your goddamn hands off of me!"

Her head spun as the sack lifted from her head. Hair stuck to her face, but the cool air filled her lungs and kissed her overheated skin, granting her immediate relief. She swayed but caught herself before lifting her hands to push the hair from her eyes. She froze at the flicker of movement beside her.

A broad figure wearing black hose and a dark green shirt with a brown doublet stood with his back toward her. A hood covered his hair and threw his profile into shadow. He reached out a gloved hand and plucked a roasted morsel from the tray.

Ruby searched the room for a weapon, any weapon. But for as plush as the room was furnished, it bore only the essentials, leaving nothing she could wield as a weapon against this madman. With her hands and feet bound, it left her at a significant disadvantage. Instead of reacting, she waited patiently hoping to lull him into underestimating her.

"How dare you take me captive." Ruby glared at the imposing man who remained encased in mystery. She scoffed. "You cannot even bear to face me. Coward."

A menacing chuckle filled the room.

The hair on her arms stood on end. Ruby shifted uncomfortably. "When the king hears of my disappearance, there will be hell to pay."

"Aye, darling Ruby. There will be blood; on that we can agree." The man turned and sat in the chair beside the table bearing the food-laden tray. With his back to the window, his face remained cast in shadows. He lounged in the chair much like Crispin on his throne. Confident and cocky to a fault.

She blinked against the bright sunlight streaming through the window. His voice. It sounded familiar, yet she could not place where she had heard it before. "I demand you release me."

He chuckled again, the sound grating and sinister. "You are in no position to make demands, sweeting."

"Who are you?" Ruby murmured, her mind spinning with questions. Irritation filled her with every passing moment in his company.

"You wound me." He pressed his gloved fist to the center of his chest. "After all these years, you do not recognize me." The gloved hand rose to the hood and pulled it back.

Brother James...Francis Seville sat before her. A twisted smile on his scarred face.

Ruby gasped; her breath stolen by the revelation. She shot to her feet and stumbled, the binding on her feet forgotten. "It cannot be." She twisted her wrists until the ropes burned her flesh. Panic gripped her and crushing pressure built deep in her chest.

He plucked another bite of roasted meat from the plate and popped it into his mouth. His cold, calculating gaze followed her.

"Why?" she gasped the word between deep breaths. Even through the onslaught of unknowns, this one simple question shone brightly above the rest. Tears pricked her eyes at the betrayal.

"I am reclaiming what is mine by birth. My crown. My kingdom. My bride." A wicked grin split his lips.

Ruby shook her head. "I refuse." Whatever hope she held faded like the summer's warmth with the approaching winter.

"This is your place now. By my side." He slowly rose to his feet and drew a dagger from the sheath on his hip.

She stumbled back when he approached her. He grasped her wrists. Ruby tried to pull away, but he tightened his grip and held her fast. Francis pressed the dagger to the tender flesh of her throat. She stilled immediately but refused to flinch at his threat and held his gaze.

"Finish it then. I would rather die than betray my king." She leaned into the dagger's blade, letting it sting as it bit her skin.

"Such spark. I have always admired that about you." He eased the blade away. "It would be far too simple to kill you." Francis gripped her throat.

Ruby sputtered and choked at the pressure. She pushed at him, trying to knock his hands away, but he held her with enough force to pin her in place while allowing her to breathe. Tears filled her eyes and fury raged through her veins.

"Mark my words carefully, Ruby. If you refuse to cooperate, I will kill every person you hold dear. Starting with your mother." His eyes glittered at her panicked inhale. "Aye, she trusts me. It will take little effort to slit her throat. Do not try my patience."

With a stilted nod, Ruby dropped her gaze. She could not let him hurt her mother. There would be no warning Marian of the impending danger. The look of determination in his gaze solidified her decision. She would do as he commanded.

"Good." He released her and took her bound hands. "Now, I release you from your bonds. You are free to move about the room. Scream all you wish. No one will hear you. My servants are loyal to me alone."

"Burn in hell." Ruby spat on him.

His grip tightened and pain coursed up her arm. She winced, and he twisted until she pressed her body against him to keep her arm from snapping like a branch. Ruby hissed and turned her face away unable to bear being this close to a treasonous serpent.

"If you persist in treating me with such disrespect, I will carve mementos from your companion then have them brought to your chamber and placed on the mantle." His hot breath washed over her cheek, leaving her feeling tainted and diseased. "Do not try my patience."

"Deceiver. You have no companion of mine." Ruby snapped even though she heard the agonized cry earlier.

"Henry will suffer for your stubbornness in blood. Limb by limb until there is nothing left." His threat hung heavy in the air.

A sob lodged in Ruby's throat. There was no mistaking the glint of evil in his eyes. He would relish the opportunity to bring pain. How had she missed it before? The kindhearted monk was gone, replaced by a bloodthirsty villain.

She softened in defeat, unable to form a response to his cruel threat. If she pushed him, he would retaliate of that she could be certain. At her nod, he cut the rope at her wrists.

"You may unbind your feet once I leave." He grasped her chin in his gloved hand. "Remember, you belong to me now."

Ruby jerked from his grasp. "You may have my body, but you will have nothing more."

"We shall see." He crossed the room intent to leave her when she called out to him.

"Why go to this trouble? You could have taken the throne with the blessing of the Privy Council." A tear slipped down her cheek. She swiped it away.

"I want Crispin to suffer, and I want the kingdom to watch him burn." Without further explanation, he walked out of the room, leaving her to stare after him in stunned silence.

Chapter Three

The longer Crispin stared at the faded map spread across the table the more his mood darkened. Two days had passed with no information on the whereabouts of Henry or Ruby.

The soldiers scoured the forests. His personal guard searched the road where they had been ambushed. Nothing remained of the wagon or the men who attacked them. Connor's report of the event had been detailed, but his men found no evidence of the incident.

His gaze rested on Ruby's jeweled scabbard. 'Twas the only item found during the search, but it gave no indication as to where she had been taken or by whom. There was no messenger with a note of ransom or demands in exchange for their return. An ominous silence filled the void, leaving the castle in a state of unrest.

Crispin paced the floor and ran his hand through his hair. Sleep eluded him and exhaustion replaced whatever frustration remained. He would not rest until he found them.

He paused at the window and leaned against the sill. A group of riders entered the gate then disappeared from view into the expansive bailey below. Judging by their pace, they returned with no new information.

Too many possibilities filled his mind. Who would dare steal his queen? Why? Crispin understood he fostered no goodwill in some of the neighboring kingdoms. And even among his own court, murmured conversations often painted him in an unfavorable light. Once the people discovered the truth of Francis's return and the disappearance of his beloved queen, a restlessness would rise from the peasantry and farmers throughout the kingdom.

He returned to the map and beat his fist against the table in a rhythmic cadence, losing himself in thought. The map before him blurred, the ink fading into a distorted mass. His focus slipped deeper into darkness. He pinched his eyes closed and swore.

"Am I interrupting?" His mother's soothing voice filled the room and eased his rising agitation.

Crispin flicked the map and pushed away from the table. "There is nothing to interrupt. I have no leads, no direction." He flexed his hands. "Perhaps I should join in the search. There must be something they missed." His gaze lingered on the forest beyond the window.

"What good would it do to put you in harm's way?" his mother asked. Her words offered a voice of reason, countering the chaos churning like a storm in his mind.

"If I were out there, I would have found them." His conviction faltered at the weak declaration.

"Crispin." She rested her hand on his arm. The tension slowly drained from his body, but the underlying emotion refused to dim. "You cannot simply charge off into the thick of battle when we have no idea who our enemy is."

He scoffed. "What would you have me do? Sit on my arse and pray for a miracle?"

"Of course not." She regarded him with the same patience one would a temperamental child. Crispin raised a brow and waited for her to continue. "I simply wish for you to use discernment before barging headlong into a fight you are ill-equipped to win."

"What do you suggest?" Crispin threw his hands up and strode across the room, impatience driving his feet into motion. His voice grew louder with passion. "I have every soldier and knight in the kingdom searching. There is no sign of the Balmont clan, whom I have no doubt played a role in Henry and Ruby's disappearance. Why else would the attackers not kill Henry?"

"Do you truly believe the Balmonts would align themselves against you?" His mother sat in the chair beside the table and folded her hands in her lap.

"They disguised themselves as raiders and attacked the

caravan carrying Ruby as a child. They were given instructions to *kill* Ruby. When they realized they failed in their original mission, they fled not only the capital, but their family holding as well." Crispin gritted his teeth, fury building like a hungry flame inside him. "Only guilt would drive them to flee with such haste."

Her expression sobered. "Is this why you and Henry left after the wedding?"

"Aye." He rested his hands on the mantle. "We spoke with every holding, every member of court in the land. They had vanished, which makes them more capable than I anticipated."

"Do you truly believe they have some part of this plot?"

"I know not whom I can trust at this point," Crispin confessed. "I fear there is no one in which I can place my faith to ensure the safety and security of not only the kingdom but those I hold dear."

"You cannot be expected to do it all yourself, my dear."

He pushed away from the mantle and faced her. The concern in her gaze nearly broke his resolve. "Then what am I to do? I cannot wait. There must be action. Retribution. Whoever did this must suffer my wrath."

"Take a moment. Clear your mind." She inhaled deeply and rested her hand against her heart. "Let us consider this logically."

Crispin would have laughed had he not seen the sincerity in her measured breaths. Instead of imitating her, he rested his hand on his hip and waited for her to open her eyes. When she finally met his gaze, she rose to her feet and crossed to where he stood. He stilled when she placed her hand over his heart.

"If they captured Ruby and Henry, then there is a strong possibility wherever they are, they are together."

"I have already considered this, Mother." He frowned. "What benefit does this serve in locating them?"

"They are together, which means they are not alone. There is hope."

"Or the bastard holding them will use one against the other to force compliance." Crispin tore himself away from her touch and paced to the opposite side of the room.

"Have you questioned the servants?"

Crispin spun to face her. "I have asked anyone with any information to come forward."

"And have they?" Her brow arched.

He shook his head.

"Then perhaps you should interview each one, starting with Ruby's personal servants." His mother crossed to the table and glanced at the map. "That young Mina is quite observant. Whoever orchestrated this knew exactly where and when to strike."

"Are you insinuating the traitor lies within these walls?" Crispin's blood heated at the thought.

"I believe they were privy to information one could only obtain through observing those inside the castle." Her fingers traced the king's road leading north from the castle. "There is a spy in our midst, my son. If we uncover them, we may find clues to lead us to the culprit."

"A spy." Crispin bristled at the possibility. "What fool would place a spy in our midst?"

"One who is no fool." His mother murmured beneath her breath. She lifted her gaze to meet his. "'Tis possible this person has been in our midst since before your father—" Her voice went silent at the mention of the former king.

Guilt nagged at Crispin. Even though he held no affection for his father and toyed with the idea of removing him from the throne, he never considered the extending implications of such a plan. There was no way to prove if it had succeeded or if someone else had. His mother's observation held weight. Whoever this spy was, they had been watching and waiting for the opportunity to present itself. A sinister possibility appeared in his mind.

"What of Francis?" Crispin mused, gauging his mother's reaction. "His reemergence seems to be quite timely, do you not agree?"

Her eyes narrowed. "You truly believe your brother has something to do with this?"

"He conveniently remained hidden from the world, shut away in the monastery, lying in wait. His position gave him the perfect opportunity to befriend Ruby."

His mother laughed. "Honestly, Crispin. How could he have possibly known her identity? Not a soul knew, even Ruby herself knew nothing of her birth parents or the betrothal agreement."

'Twas true. There was no way of him knowing. However, fate played a hand in their meeting, of that he was certain.

"It does not change this miraculous revelation." He tapped his fingers on the table. "And his refusal to abdicate aligns perfectly with their disappearance."

"Such a betrayal is not in your brother's nature. Francis would never use such tactics for his own purpose. What would it serve him? If he truly wanted the throne, he would only have to petition the privy council. What benefit would he have to pursue such an elaborate charade?" Vivienne rounded the table to face him squarely.

"To spite me." Crispin's response echoed through the room with the crack of a whip. "To make me suffer."

Her gaze softened, and she cupped his cheek. Crispin closed his eyes at the touch but remained firmly committed to his statement.

"Must you always believe the worst of mankind?" She rubbed her thumb along his jaw. "I know not what vile poison has turned your heart, but if you nurture this beast, then you will experience only pain and suffering."

Crispin refused to react to her observation even though it bit into his soul with a sharp, well-aimed blade. He placed his hand over hers and slowly removed it. "Say what you will, but Francis has a hand in this. I shall prove it, and then you will see the truth of your sainted son."

Pain flickered in her eyes. "As you wish, your majesty." She turned and retreated from his presence before he could rescind his harsh words.

"Damn it!" He pounded his fists on the table tearing the corner of the map. Replacing the torn edge, he traced the path of the king's road as it wound through the country.

Crispin vowed to uncover the truth, no matter the cost. He

would find his queen. Then he would gut the villain responsible for his pain and hang them out for the crows to feast upon.

Chapter Four

Ruby rested her head against the window staring out over the treetops to the mountains beyond. In the distance they rose up to the heavens, the white-capped tips disappearing into the clouds. They were certainly in the north, but if they were within the boundaries of Meradin, Ruby could not tell. She had never traveled this far north.

A falcon drifted through the air, diving down and disappearing into the withering leaves clinging to the trees. She pushed away the sudden longing rising in her chest. If only she could send a message to Crispin.

The female servants arrived twice daily, bearing her morning and evening meals. But they were never alone. Two armed guards stood sentry by the door while they placed the tray on the table and exited without a word. No matter how intently Ruby tried to engage them in conversation, they ignored her as though she were not even present.

There was no possibility of convincing them to relay a message for her, let alone begging for them to aid in her escape. She spent the remainder of her time cloistered in the gilded cage surrounded by soft trappings and pretty ornaments.

After tearing the room apart searching for something she could wield as a weapon, Ruby embraced the futility of the endeavor. Francis, it seemed, anticipated her actions in every possible way. Such knowledge burrowed beneath her skin and left her uncomfortable.

How long had he lain in wait for the opportune moment to spring his well-positioned trap? The logistics alone made her head ache, let alone the plotting and scheming. There were too many questions and never any answers.

Francis had not visited her since the first day when he

revealed his role in her capture. She loathed the idea of spending any amount of time in his presence, and yet her curiosity burned for satisfaction. What possessed a man to turn on his family and allies, everything he once stood for?

Ruby could make no sense of his actions. She cursed herself for a fool, placing her trust in him, feeding upon his lies and deception. It left her stomach twisting. The disgust manifested physically, leaving her ill and clutching her stomach. She worried not only for her safety but that of her unborn child. She spent the nights lying curled beneath the plush linens, surrounded by darkness, staring at the curtains hanging around the bed.

No one would come. She was utterly alone.

Even the blossom of hope in knowing Henry was close withered with every passing day. No screams. No shouts. Nothing but silence penetrated her gaudy prison.

The time spent here blended together. Four days passed since she first woke in this room, but there was no way to know how long she had been incapacitated.

She rubbed the welt on the back of her head where they had struck her. A wave of shame mixed with a sharp pain in her side made her double over.

Pacing the room, Ruby attempted to redirect her focus on possible ways she could escape. No matter how many times she glanced out the window, she could not change the distance to the ground. Even should she wish to risk escape in such a manner, a fall from such a height, while it would not kill her, would certainly endanger the life she carried.

Her hand rested protectively over her stomach. This would not defeat her. She would persist and in doing so ensure the safety of her child. If Francis had wanted her dead, he would have put a blade to her throat and ended it. He would not take careful effort to feed and shelter her. Although she could not fathom his reason for doing so.

She would not concede defeat. He held no control over her. No matter how much he threatened those she cared about, she would find a way to fight him. But a frontal assault would never work. Nay, she would need to devise another method to defeat him, but what? And how?

The twist of a key in the lock pulled her from the depth of her thoughts. She spun away from the window.

The door swung open revealing the female servant in her simple garb bearing a tray with her evening meal, a steaming mug of tea, and a goblet of wine.

Ruby's gaze shifted to the two guards blocking the door. Their vacant eyes followed her as she moved to the small table where the servant placed the tray.

"Grammercy." She smiled at the servant.

The woman caught her gaze. A flash of fear filled her red-rimmed eyes before she blinked and quickly turned away. Ruby's heart ached at the sight of such panic and uncertainty. Although she could certainly understand the woman's position. Perhaps Francis relied too heavily on fear than endearing those in his service to ensure their compliance and loyalty.

The two guards stepped aside, allowing the woman to leave, but they did not close the door. Ruby ignored the food and strained to see beyond the two guards. Their unwavering stance offered no aid, and Ruby slumped in disappointment. But still, they did not close the door.

Before she could open her mouth, the two brutes stepped aside revealing Francis. Gone were his monk's robes, replaced with fine garments fashioned for a king. Ruby's stomach churned at the sight of the royal insignia embroidered on his doublet.

Francis entered without invitation and dismissed the guards with a wave of his hand. They closed the door, leaving her alone with him.

Ruby placed the table between them. Should he wish to harm her, he could do so, but she would fight him regardless. She tipped her chin up and faced him without intimidation.

"What do you want?" Ruby snapped, fighting off the revulsion of his presence.

"It would be remiss of me to neglect my honored guest." He gestured to the tray of food. "Sit. Eat."

Whatever hunger she harbored before now faded. Ruby shook her head. "I would rather starve."

Francis tutted and took the seat nearest the door. "If not for yourself, then what of the child?"

She gripped the bedpost attempting to suppress the fury rising inside her. "What do you care what happens to me or the child? You captured me against my will and locked me away." Venom spewed from her lips in pure defiance. "Why not just end my suffering? Kill me. Kill the king. Take your throne and then burn in hell."

"Come now, Ruby." He cocked his head and smiled. "Where would the challenge be if I killed you?" He plucked the goblet from the tray and drank deeply from the ostentatious cup.

"Give me a sword, and I'll show you a challenge." Ruby clutched her side as a spasm took hold. She straightened quickly as to not show weakness in his presence. He would not win. Not while a breath remained in her body.

"Such passion is an admirable trait in a queen." Francis set the cup aside and rose to his feet. "I shall enjoy taming your tongue when we are wed."

"Wed?" A snort escaped her. "I would rather die with honor than surrender to a serpent like you."

Francis crossed the room in a burst of speed she had not anticipated. Ruby stumbled out of reach until her back slammed into the wall. His breath reeked of wine. She turned her head unable to stomach the pungent aroma.

"What you desire is immaterial." He traced his gloved finger along her throat. Bile rose in her throat. "I am your master now, and when I take the throne, you shall take your place beside me. Willingly or not, 'tis where you belong. I will bring you to heel regardless of your personal feelings."

"You underestimate me." Ruby faced him, reclaiming the defiance that served her faithfully for so long. "The moment you turn your back on me, I will drive a blade through your blackened heart."

"I would expect nothing less from the Lady of the Forest." His gaze narrowed before he caught her chin in his deceptively strong grip. Ruby struggled against his hold, but he pinned her to the wall with his broad body. The monk's robes had hidden his muscular form. It seemed she had been the one to underestimate him. Shame filled her.

"You realize the futility of such an action. The throne is mine by right." His sneer radiated arrogant confidence. He encircled her throat with a firm grip. "You were betrothed to me long before you ever wielded a sword. Therefore, you are mine."

Ruby choked at the pressure. Her eyes watered as she gasped for breath trying to pry his hand off. When he finally released her, she wheezed and coughed. He stepped away, and she rushed forward, knocking into the tray as she reached for the mug of tea.

The mild aroma tickled her nose, but the warmth soothed her throat as she drank.

"Good girl. Drink up. Save your strength." He laughed as he strode to the door. "You will need it."

The sound unnerved her. "Burn in hell."

Ruby doubled over when a sharp pain pierced her abdomen. She cried out and stumbled forward, falling to the floor. Fire burned through her belly. She clutched her arms around herself and screamed as the agony overwhelmed her.

Francis stood over her watching in amusement. She glared at him before another piercing cramp overtook her senses.

"What have you done to me?" She whimpered between breaths. "Poison?"

The once friendly smile she considered warm and comforting twisted in horrific pleasure. "Nothing quite so drastic. I need you hale and hearty when I take the throne." He tisked. "But I cannot have a bastard threatening my well-laid plans."

Horror filled her. "Oh, saints above. Please." Pain shot through her once more. She screamed in agony. Her heart ripped from her chest as her body revolted against the one thing she wished to protect. Her child.

"Finally." He chuckled. "A pinch of pennyroyal with each meal. Herbs can heal, but they can also serve other purposes."

Ruby whimpered and clung to consciousness with a single thread. Fire radiated from her womb. Tears filled her eyes.

"I cannot have that bastard vying for my throne." His footsteps recede and the door opens. "Once it is removed, I will replace it with my own." He closed the door behind him.

Left in silence and agony, Ruby writhed on the floor and prayed. When the blood came, she wept.

Chapter Five

Not a soul dared meet his gaze as he passed. Servants cowered, hiding their faces and bowing low, in an obvious effort to appease their king's temper. Crispin strode down the corridor, ignoring the whispers left in his wake.

Five days passed since Ruby and Henry had been taken. Five sleepless nights filled with churning rage and unsatisfied questions. Not one returning soldier bore news worth hearing. Even Ruby's maids were of little use. The younger being quite innocent, and the other having abandoned her post in the chaos surrounding her mistress' disappearance. He fought against the desire to charge out of the gates and find Ruby himself, but that would do nothing but excite speculation and incite instability.

Instead, he sent his soldiers with a summons for his brother at the monastery. There was a connection between the queen's capture and his brother's magnanimous announcement before the privy council. Although he bore no proof of it, he felt their corresponding ties deep in the pit of his gut.

The young page blundered along behind him barely able to keep up. According to the lad, his guards returned with important information concerning Francis and awaited him in the throne room. Crispin hoped to find his brother bound and on his knees begging for forgiveness.

He burst through the doors leading to the throne room. A cluster of armored knights turned, dropping to their knees at the sight of their king. Crispin acknowledged them with a nod of his head, his attention focused instead on what lay apparently absent.

"Where is he?" Crispin's fury stoked to life.

"My liege." The head knight stepped forward, his head bowed in subservience, but his words rang clear through the room. "We searched the monastery. There was no sign of him. The monks claim he stole away the night he returned."

Crispin grit his teeth. "Where has he gone?"

The knight shook his head. "They knew nothing of his intent nor his direction. His final words proclaimed he is on a mission from God."

His shouted curse shook the rafters. To their merit, the knights did not blink or cower at his outburst. The page, however, trembled like a mouse cornered by a vicious cat. Crispin ignored the weakness and instead turned the possibilities over in his mind.

"Francis disappears the night before my bride and my most loyal Right Hand are taken in an ambush. This is no coincidence." He growled before turning back to the knight. "Take your men to each village and question every soul. Leave no stone unturned. He cannot have vanished into the wind without a trace. Follow the trail."

The knights bowed once more before taking their leave. Crispin dismissed the page and waiting servants. He paced the length of the throne room in silence. What underhanded game was Francis playing?

Irritated by this unwelcome turn of events, Crispin returned to his chamber and poured himself a glass of wine. The chill of the oncoming winter left its delicate print on the window glass. He settled in the oversized chair before the fire and lost himself in the flames.

The uneasy ache of loss twisted around his heart. He refused to relinquish hope. While he yet drew breath, he would not rest. He would find Ruby. If Henry were taken with her, then he would find them both. The bond tying him to them intensified this restlessness. He disliked being helpless. Not knowing whether they were alive or dead and unable to mount a rescue and save them.

Bitterness tarnished his thoughts. Francis, for all his pretty words and humility, lay coiled like an adder in the tall grass waiting to strike. It seemed Crispin was alone in this assessment of his long-lost brother. His council and his own mother were convinced of Francis's sincerity. This knowledge left him adrift in the confinement of his mind.

Darkness settled beyond the glass. Three goblets of wine gave Crispin a reprieve from the endless torment of the inescapable horror surrounding him. The warmth of the fire and comfort of the wine compounded the exhaustion weighing heavily upon him. His eyes drifted closed and he slipped into the welcoming embrace of sleep.

A chill reached through the haze of his dreams and beneath the fabric of his sleeves, sliding across his bare arms. He woke with a shiver, finding the room cloaked in shadow. The fire burned down to embers in the hearth.

Unease surrounded him. His heartbeat echoed in the silence. Crispin reached for his dagger, but the sheath lay empty against his thigh. He bolt upright and scanned the darkness.

"Who goes there?" The question slipped from his lips making him question his own sanity. But he knew without a doubt, he was not alone.

A piercing light appeared in the corner of the room. Holding a shuttered lantern, the cloaked intruder stepped forward.

Unarmed, Crispin braced himself for an attack. "Speak your purpose."

The intruder pulled back the hood. Ruby's maid, Ivy, stood before him, her green eyes sparkling in the dim light.

"What is the meaning of this?" He hissed, taking a step closer. His steps faltered, and he gripped the chair to keep himself upright. "What have you done to me?"

"A little something to help you sleep." She set the lantern on the table against the wall. The glint of gold in her other hand revealed his dagger.

"You poisoned me?" He glared at the wench.

"Nothing fatal." A smile tugged at her lips. "Had I wished you dead, I would have succeeded with very little effort." She gestured to the chair. "Sit down before you fall over."

Crispin gripped the chair tighter balking in pure stubbornness. "I will not take orders from a common whore."

Ivy's jaw clenched. "If you wish to know where your precious Ruby is being held, then you will bite your tongue and follow my instructions."

Rage filled his vision with shades of spilled blood. "Where is she? What have you done with her, traitorous bitch?"

"What makes you think I had any part of her capture?" The woman seemed unshaken by his anger which infuriated him more.

Crispin took measured steps toward her. His gaze remained unwavering even though his legs threatened to give out from beneath him. "I doubt it mere coincidence upon learning of her disappearance, you abandoned your post. I have it on good authority you have a penchant for vanishing from the castle for days on end. If you are so quick to neglect your duties, perhaps it took very little to convince you to betray your queen."

Her countenance flickered with indecision. Crispin seized the opportunity and lunged forward. He grasped her wrists with both hands and twisted. She cried out in surprise but did not relinquish the weapon.

They struggled, ramming into the chairs and overturning the table, spilling wine across the floor. She slipped in the liquid, and he seized her around the waist, slamming her into the wall. The maid clawed at his face with one hand as he attempted to wrench the dagger from the other fist.

He beat her clenched hand against the stone until the gold dagger slipped from her fingers and clattered to the floor. Heart beating wildly in his chest, Crispin leaned his weight against her, pinning his arm against her throat.

Ivy relinquished the fight. Her body remained tense beneath him, and Crispin refused to give her the opportunity to turn against him. He underestimated her once before, she would not get the opportunity to do so again.

"Where is she?" Crispin growled, his breaths harsh and uneven. The effects of whatever herb she used in his wine left lingering effects. He pushed through them and focused instead on the traitor at his mercy.

"I know not where they took her," she hissed, gasping

against the pressure of his arm on her throat.

"They?" Crispin pressed harder until she choked. "If you do not tell me by choice, then I will extract the information by force." He eased back enough to allow her to speak.

"I do not know who took her or where." She gripped his arm, digging her nails into his flesh when he applied the pressure again. "But I know how to find them."

Crispin stepped back and snatched the dagger from the floor. Ivy doubled over, gripping her throat and coughing. In an instant, he snatched her by the hair and threw her into the nearest chair. He ignored her pointed glare and held the blade to her neck.

"Do you take me for a fool?" he murmured, savoring the look of hatred and fear in her lovely eyes. Oh aye, this wench could worm her way into the hearts of any man she chose, bending them to her will. Such an enticing morsel. The perfect cover for treason. "Which poor soul did you corrupt? Hmmm?"

"I know not—"

"Such pretty lies," Crispin hissed. "You have the ear of the queen as her personal servant, but that alone is not enough to secure your safety within these walls." Recognition rekindled the fire in her gaze. "Whom did you seduce? One of my guards? A knight at arms? Did they promise you protection and profess their undying love?" Crispin twisted the dagger, drawing a droplet of blood from her pale skin.

She did not flinch. No cry of pain. No tears. No pleas or begging. The woman was either reckless or stupid. Crispin shook his head pushing both thoughts aside. She showed no fear at his promise of violence. Her gaze held his with challenge and determination as though she accepted her fate, or worse, gambled with it. If she had something to do with Ruby's capture, then she would have required a way to escape retribution should it come back to her.

"Henry," Crispin murmured the name upon the realization. "You seduced him with your lithe body and your sinful tongue." He dug the blade harder against her throat. A trickle of blood ran over her breast and disappeared into her bodice.

He caught a glimpse of what could have been regret before she hid behind a mask of indifference. "I have my orders."

"What orders? From whom?" He tightened his hold on her hair. She winced at the motion.

"Henry caught me stealing from your presence chamber. The queen offered me redemption in exchange for my loyalty."

Confusion muddled his mind. What madness did she speak? Neither Henry nor Ruby brought him this news. Were they conspiring against him? Such thoughts paved a dangerous path. The two souls he trusted and loved beyond anything on this mortal plane uncovered a traitor in his castle and chose not to tell him of it. Impossible.

"Such lies will be your last." The temptation to draw the blade across her throat battled with his resolve to draw the truth from her traitorous lips.

"I speak the truth. The queen released me with the understanding I would lead her to the man who purchased me from the Guild."

He clenched tighter. "The Guild is a myth."

"I know nothing but the Guild. They raised me. Trained me. They are no myth, but they work only in shadow." Her voice rose in pitch as he tilted her head into an unnatural position. "I was sold to a faceless master."

"A faceless master? A phantom cult?" Crispin scoffed. He removed the blade and released her with a rough shove. "You truly think I am a fool to believe such sensational tales."

Ivy pressed her gloved hand to her bloody throat. "'Tis the truth. I have never seen his face. He leaves instructions in the forest, and I respond in the same manner. We have never met, but he holds my contract."

"What of your free will?" Crispin taunted with a sneer.

"I know no other life." She dropped her gaze to the overturned chair. "Should I fail, I will be killed. There is no free will for such as me."

"Then why choose to barter with the queen?" He clenched the dagger in his fist prepared to use it should he need to do so.

"The queen has shown me nothing but kindness. I owe her

a debt." Her solemn words settled in the silent room with finality. "Kill me if you must, but you must rescue the queen. I forfeit my life for hers."

Crispin trusted her even less than he had when she revealed she tampered with his wine, but he could not allow his beloved treasure to suffer at the hands of some faceless monster. These words could be nothing more than well-crafted tales to spur him into action. Regardless, he could not sit on his arse and do nothing. Too much time elapsed with nothing to show for their efforts. Such dire circumstances required a change in tactic. He regarded the maid for a long moment before exhaling sharply and sheathing his dagger.

"You will take me to the place where you leave communication for your *master*." Resolve bolstered him into action. "We shall discover his identity and demand he lead us to the queen."

The maid rose to her feet tentatively.

Crispin gripped her jaw in his hand and forced her to meet his gaze. "If you are leading me on a merry chase, so help me God, I will ensure your final days are filled with endless pain and suffering."

Her jerky nod solidified her understanding.

"Come," he commanded, roughly taking her by the arm and steering her toward the wardrobe. "Help me dress. I have no intention of allowing you to leave my sight."

She obeyed, but Crispin refused to give her an opportunity to draw a weapon on him again. One thing soothed his apprehension. He was closer to finding Ruby than he had been before. Ignited by the promise of finding her, hope burned like an ember in his chest and drove him to action.

Chapter Six

Screams echoed into the night. Henry laid in wretched silence unable to move further than the restraints would allow. Hours had passed noted by the decay of the sunlight into darkness. His untreated injuries ached, and his tongue burned with a desperate thirst. But his focus remained not on himself but the haunting sobs which seemed to surround him. Pain lanced through him with every agonizing cry.

The first one pierced his soul. He fought against his restraints until blood coated his hands and ankles, but to no avail, he could not come to her aid. There was no mercy granted from his captors.

Henry would kill him. Rip him apart with his bare hands in retribution for the torment he inflicted upon Ruby.

Shrouded in darkness, Henry rose to sit on the edge of the bed. The tremor in his hands worsened.

Another heart-wrenching scream drove him to his feet.

"Leave her, you bastards!" Henry shouted profanities and vows of vengeance until his voice grew hoarse. He swayed at the effort. Fear and fury combined, feeding the depleted reserves barely keeping him upright.

Her screams faded into a haunting silence. Henry panicked. Had they finally killed her?

His shouts renewed with intensity. Fresh blood warmed his hands as he pulled against his bonds.

No response met his frenzied calls. He failed her. Relinquished to the hands of the enemy, she suffered because of his inability to protect her.

Henry collapsed onto the narrow cot. While his body embraced the reprieve, his mind suffered from the torment. His cracked lips parted in a pained gasp when he relaxed against the bed. Whatever fight remained bled out of him and onto the cold stone floor. His consciousness followed, surrendered to the blissful embrace of nothingness.

For the briefest moment, Henry's pain vanished. His heart remained heavy, but his physical form held none of the turmoil it bore previously. A dream. Lovely and serene, it surrounded him with peace. He stood in the field beyond the castle walls. In the distance, Ruby rode her mare through the open green meadow. Hair unbound and a smile upon her lips.

Crispin stood beside him, watching his queen gallop through the field like a goddess bound in sunshine and radiance.

Ivy appeared behind him. Her arms wrapped around his waist, her fingers sliding over his doublet. Just as they reached his belt, a storm rose over the horizon.

Lightning flashed overhead. Ruby and Crispin disappeared. A crack of thunder split the stillness. Ivy vanished. Henry spun around as the sky opened and rain poured from the heavens.

The scene faded into a haze and plunged into darkness. Pain slammed into him with the force of a destrier's kick. He gasped and clutched his chest.

Cool liquid coated his face, filling his nose and mouth. He coughed and sputtered attempting to escape the onslaught. *Water.* His body relished the refreshment, but his lips burned at the contact. He rolled away to escape the sensation of drowning. What little spit he had dribbled to the floor as he hung off the bed.

When he opened his eyes, a pair of boots filled his vision. He blinked to clear his sight. Well-tailored leather.

A hand gripped his neck forcing him back. It grasped his jaw and pried it open before pouring water from a pitcher into his open mouth. Henry struggled against the hold, even though he wished to quench his thirst, there was too much.

He wrenched free and turned away again, his body heaving at the assault.

"Enough!" he sputtered, spitting on the floor.

Relief filled him at the sound of retreating footsteps. Henry waited for the sound of the door closing, but it never came.

A soft glow filled the room.

Henry glanced up, lifting his hand to block the brightness of the lantern. His eyes adjusted and hatred congealed in the pit of his stomach.

"You killed her." He glowered at his captor hidden in the shadows. "Now you have come to finish me off. Do it. Take your blade to my throat and end my suffering."

The figure regarded him a moment without even the slightest inkling of remorse or mercy. "You always were so dramatic, Henry. Forever playing the martyr of selfless sacrifice."

Henry hung his head and pinched his eyes closed. "You have won. What more do you want?"

"This is far from over." His captor hung the lantern and stepped into the light.

Francis.

Indignation filled him. Henry struggled, wasting what little strength remained in fighting against unmovable iron chains. "You son of a bitch! Lying coward. Crispin was right to distrust you."

Francis tutted, meeting his gaze steadily. "Is that any way to speak to the rightful King of Meradin?" The flicker of the lantern light lent his eyes a sinister glow.

"You are not my king," Henry spat. "You will never be king."

"I am, and I will." He tapped his gloved fingers on the hilt of his dagger.

"You may as well kill me now." The fury simmered beneath his skin. "I will do everything in my power to stop you."

"Death would be far too simple for either of you. Oh no, this is only the first battle in a long siege. And you both have your roles to play." Francis sneered, the scars on his face pulling tight.

"What have you done to Ruby?" Henry growled.

"I have rooted out the evil." Those glowing eyes intensified. "Removed the abomination growing in her womb."

"Oh, God," Henry muttered as the horrific implication of his confession registered in his mind. The screams of agony. The sobbing. He whispered a prayer. Ruby suffered alone, and there was nothing he could do to offer comfort or hope.

"In time, I shall replace it with the true heir to the kingdom of Meradin." Francis's ominous words filled Henry with revulsion. His stomach clenched and roiled. Had there been anything within it, it would have spilled forth.

"She placed her faith in you, and you betrayed her. You betrayed us all." Horror flooded him. "What kind of monster have you become? What has twisted your soul to engage in such evil?"

"I am as I have always been." His mocking laugh echoed through the narrow cell. "You chose to see what you wished to see, not what was truly before you."

Memories assailed Henry. Visions of them training. In celebration. In grief. In battle. Together, as a group, Henry, Crispin, Francis, Simon, Jacob, and Timothy. Inseparable, undefeated, feasting on their glorious accolades. But Francis was always the golden heir. The hope and pride of all Meradin. Had he fooled them all? Hiding the truth of his dark and twisted soul from those closest to him with such clever manipulation.

"You were never cruel, Francis." Henry shook his head. "Whatever happened that night, it warped your soul."

"That fire stole everything from me!" Francis hissed, his scarred face twisted in hatred. It softened a fraction as he attempted to control his emotions. Henry saw the battle raging within him, reflected in the depths of those familiar eyes. "But it was also a rebirth."

Henry stared at him in disbelief. "We mourned you. All of us. Crispin bore the brunt of the guilt for your demise."

"Crispin is no saint, no hero. He bears no grief or guilt for my fate," Francis snapped.

With all his might, Henry lunged off the bed at his captor. The chains snapped tight, jerking him to the floor. He collided with the stones in a heap, pain shooting through his limbs.

Francis's laughter filled the room. "Save your strength. You will need it for what is coming."

The soft glow of the lantern led Francis from the cell. He

closed the door behind him. Laughter echoed down the corridor beyond the door mocking him.

Henry lay on the cool floor, letting it warm his overheated face. How could he have been so blind? So foolish? Had he not been distracted with Ivy, he would have been able to see through Francis's lies? But who would have believed him?

Crispin would have. He saw through the deception the very moment Henry brought Francis back to the castle.

He beat his head against the stone as a sob welled up in his chest. Henry could have stopped him. But his lust distracted him from his vow to protect the king and queen. Now they all suffered the consequences of his failings.

Hope had not vanished completely. It glowed like a beacon on the distant horizon. Ruby was alive. Francis had no intention to kill them outright. He required them to play a role in his plans.

A smile curled his cracked lips making him wince. Aye, there was still hope.

Francis's words rang clear in his mind. Henry would save his strength. He would need it to cut the bastard's traitorous throat.

Chapter Seven

While the servants followed his instructions without question, they cast curious glances at Ivy who followed in his wake. Their eyes widened when they spied the shackles binding her wrists and the chain he held in his fist.

Ivy said little as he made preparations. As it should be. She was his servant and now his prisoner. He knew nothing of her past connections or her intent. The answers she gave him were evasive and left him even more skeptical.

They waited near the postern gate for the groom the bring around the horses. He wished to keep their little adventure a secret for as long as possible. If it were revealed the king decided to follow a traitor into the woods to find his stolen queen, there would be chaos.

The woman beside him shifted, making the chain clink against his thigh. Ivy stood wordlessly behind him, but her gaze fixed on a point beyond his shoulder.

When he turned, he hoped to find the groom leading the horses. Instead, he found his mother staring at him from the small doorway off the kitchen. He recognized the patronizing expression on her lovely face as he had seen it often over the duration of his life.

She lifted her skirts delicately and approached.

Crispin gripped the chain to get Ivy's attention. "Remain silent."

Ivy tilted her head in acknowledgment, dropping her gaze.

"You intend to leave without explaining yourself." Her statement was an admonishment, not an inquiry.

"I must see to this personally." Crispin squared his shoulders. "I shall return in a few days."

His mother's loving eyes narrowed as they fell on Ivy and

the chain linking them before pinning him with a questioning stare. "If I did not know better, I would say you are avoiding your responsibilities in order to engage in a fruitless search for Ruby." She folded her hands and regarded him carefully. "However, we have nearly exhausted every possible recourse to recover both her and Henry."

Crispin arched his brow in surprise but recovered quickly. "I have new information which could lead me to them. I cannot entrust it to anyone and must see it through."

At his mother's reluctant nod, Crispin relaxed, and confidence infused him.

"I shall convey your apologies to the privy council." She inclined her head. "What shall I tell them when they ask why their king has taken such a task upon his own shoulders?"

"When those they love are ripped from their grasp and their lives burned to ash, only then will they understand the depths of my commitment." Indignation burned hot in his gut. "I shall deal with them upon my return."

"Very well." His mother offered a smile, but it did not reach her eyes. A lingering sadness filled them when the groom approached, leading his dapple-gray gelding, Ghost. She watched in silence as he placed the leather bags over the back of the saddle and mounted the horse. When he pulled Ivy into the saddle before him, his mother's expression hardened.

"I shall return. Mark my words." He gathered the reins in his gloved hand and secured the chain to his saddle. "You must watch the kingdom in my absence."

"May God grant you mercy, my son." She stepped back as he nudged the gelding into motion.

Crispin resisted the urge to take one last glimpse of his mother before slipping through the postern gate. As the distance between them and the castle grew, the uncertainty faded into a dull ache. A newfound confidence imbued his soul.

Ivy shifted, rubbing against him.

He clapped his hand on her thigh and growled. "You will remain still, wench, and mark my words if you attempt to turn on me, I will not hesitate to slit that pretty throat."

The woman stilled and remained silent.

Once upon a time, such a tempting morsel would have driven him to distraction. He would have taken what she offered. Even going as far as accepting her challenge as a form of flirtation. But now, the press of her body against his filled him with disgust. He longed for only one woman. Ruby put all others to shame with her wit, fire, and beauty.

As they continued deeper into the forest, Crispin allowed his mind to wander. There was nothing he wished to say to his unwelcome companion, nor was there anything he desired to hear from her poisoned lips other than the truth of the plot against him.

Crispin could not fault Henry for taking an interest in the woman. Ignoring her treasonous intent, any man would find her enticing enough for some bed sport. Henry dedicated his life to the kingdom, to his service. He deserved a well-earned fuck with a lovely wench. No one would fault him for wanting her.

"There." She pointed to a winding trail breaking off from the main road. It veered in the direction of the lake. One could hardly call it a road with the overgrown brush and low-hanging branches.

With a creeping unease, Crispin urged the horse down the disused path. It had been years since he wandered these old trails. He and Henry had once taken a trail similar to this which led to a cliffside overhanging the lake. They stripped and dove into the refreshing waters, nearly dying from their careless actions. Invigorating, certainly, but not wise. His mother had scolded them harshly when she discovered their little adventure.

Simon, Timothy, Jacob, and Francis had followed them. Sweet, sainted Francis could not bear the burden of silence. Crispin scowled at the memory. He ruined everything in his quest to live up to the expectations placed upon him as the golden prince of Meradin.

The deeper they ventured into the forest, the heavier the uncertainty hung upon his shoulders. He could not shake the nagging possibility he may be walking into a trap. It did not matter. He could not sit idly by while his soldiers searched for

Ruby and Henry. His grip on the reins tightened as they wove around the fallen branches. Dying leaves fell around them as they wove along the path around the lake.

Ivy sat quietly against him. Her hands rested against Ghost's mane. The silence increased his distrust of the woman who so eagerly offered information after confessing to being a spy. She was more than that. Crispin recognized the cool detachment of an assassin. Whoever trained her, owned her loyalty, and they invested heavily. Only a fool would cast aside such an asset with little care.

He did not trust her, and yet he followed her into this heart of darkness.

Even though the trees lay quite bare, the tangled branches and thick pines obscured the sky overhead and cast them into shadows. Dark patches of moss clung to the trees. Ghost's hooves squelched beneath him as the ground grew saturated with moisture.

The overgrowth became so thick, it became increasingly difficult for Crispin to navigate Ghost with them astride. He moved to dismount when Ivy gestured to their right.

"Just through there."

He maneuvered them through a narrow passage. On the other side, the path spilled into a small meadow surrounded by sloping hills and tall trees. A small oasis hidden in the thicket. Off to the right stood a tall, gnarled oak tucked at the base of an overhanging ridge. He could see the tree's struggle to survive warped it as the branches reached beyond the ridge toward the minimal sunlight.

As they approached, he noted the base lay as wide as the arched door leading to the throne room. The jagged branches stretched overhead like a dark, twisted crown.

Crispin dismounted and helped Ivy slide from the saddle. He gripped the chain tight to keep firm control over her. Ghost wandered toward the center of the meadow and grazed.

Ivy strode toward the ancient, gnarled oak tree. She knelt on the roots and reached into a dark, gaping hole at the base.

He scoffed. *What game is this?*

When she removed her hand, a leather-bound bundle lay clenched in her fist. She carefully opened it.

Empty. Crispin shook his head. What did he expect? A signed confession of guilt and a map?

Ivy reached into her bodice and removed a small slip of parchment. Crispin snatched it from her hand and peeled it open.

"What is this?" Crispin frowned at the unintelligible writing inside the missive.

"A coded message. I am relaying no new information and requesting direction." Ivy took the message from his hand and tucked it into the leather bag. She carefully replaced it within the tree and rose to her feet.

Crispin wrapped his hand around her throat and pinned her against the tree. Her luminescent eyes widened in surprise before narrowing. She gripped his wrist with her shackled hands.

"If you value your life, you will tell me the truth." He gritted his teeth, boring his gaze into hers as though searching for any flicker of deception in her soul. "I will not hesitate to slit your throat and leave you here for your master to find."

"Would you risk your beloved by indulging in such rash behavior?" She gasped between breaths as he clenched tighter.

Crispin dropped his hand, and she slumped back against the tree. "Do not tempt me." He spun and strode to where Ghost happily munched on the tall grass.

Ivy stumbled along behind them as he led Ghost from the hidden meadow. They carefully climbed the sloped incline to the left of the overgrown thicket. After a few minutes, they discovered a small gap in the trees.

After tying Ghost to a nearby tree, he pulled Ivy alongside him. "There." He gestured to the narrow slit in the trees. Peering inside, he grinned. The position allowed a perfect view of the small meadow and the gnarled, old oak tree where Ivy had hidden the message.

"We wait." He shoved her shoulder, and she collapsed onto a pile of leaves.

Crispin sat across from her, keeping the meadow in

constant view. He drew the satchel from around his torso and pulled some bread and dried fruit from inside.

Ivy refused to meet his gaze, even when he offered a piece of dried fruit. She snatched the offered item and stuffed it in her mouth.

'Twould be a long wait, but at least it would be in silence. Crispin doubted she would answer any of his questions with any degree of honesty.

He refused to trust her. Or anyone for that matter. Instead, he focused on the meadow, ignoring the nagging voice of warning in his mind, and the satisfaction he would feel at running his blade through the bastard who thought he could steal his greatest treasure.

Chapter Eight

Daylight blurred into darkness. Lost in the agonizing pain, Ruby succumbed to the welcome distraction of the dream world. Her tormented visions morphed into nightmares, but she no longer battled these imaginary demons. She embraced their company for they were saints compared to the devil who held her captive.

Ruby longed to remain forever, lest the waking world rip her soul to pieces once more. When the soft, warm melody infiltrated her clouded mind, she ventured toward it, slowly pulling herself from sleep.

"Mother," she murmured as she opened her eyes. The sun shone brightly through the window. She blinked against it, catching shadows out of the corner of her eyes.

The soft bedding tempted her to return to the shadowed dreams. Her arms lay heavy against her sides. Her legs remained rooted. Every part of her ached and protested. She groaned when her attempt to shift her weight into a sitting position failed. She barely budged. A spike of pain radiated through her lower abdomen and down through her hips. She licked her dry lips. The demanding thirst roused desperation inside her. She shifted again.

"Mother?" Her broken cry echoed through the room.

A stooped woman appeared by her side startling her. "Save your strength, pet. You are far too weak."

Ruby's gaze followed the old woman. Her crag-lined face bespoke her years. She moved quickly for a woman of her age, fetching a rag and a mug from the table, and returning to the bedside with purposeful movements.

"Who are you?" Ruby failed to relax when the woman dabbed the rag against her head. Cool and damp, it soothed the ache.

"We were given strict instructions," a second old woman snapped, appearing somewhere beyond Ruby's vision. Nearly a mirror image of the first. The women eyed each other with narrow gazes for a moment before the first one snapped her toothless mouth closed.

"Please." A sob warbled from deep within her chest.

The women exchanged another long look before the second frowned and threw her hands up in the air shaking her head wildly. "On your head be it."

"We are sisters. Emma." She gestured to herself and then to her sister. "Eva."

Eva harumphed in acknowledgment. "You will anger him," she hissed at her sister.

Emma tisked. "We have been his faithful servants. If he wishes her to be his queen, then we must bring the life back." She pressed the rag to Ruby's heated cheeks. Her brown eyes widened, drawing Ruby in.

"Why—" A spasm wracked her, making her cough and wheeze. Her stomach lurched. She groaned and pinched her eyes closed until the feeling passed. "Why serve him? Such evil."

"He saved us. Years ago. We are in his debt." Emma nodded sagely as though it were the only logical repayment of such an obligation. "To disobey would be to dishonor him."

Bile stung Ruby's throat. How could anyone serve such a monster?

A mug appeared before her lips. "Drink," Emma encouraged.

She struggled to incline her head enough to take a small amount of liquid in her mouth. The tepid tea washed the bitter taste from her mouth and quenched her thirst. She drank greedily. Some of the tea spilled over her chin and onto the blanket.

Emma dabbed it with the rag and smiled. "Better?"

Ruby nodded with hesitation. What did they mean to do to her? Befriend her and relay her secrets back to Francis? Poison her?

The memory flashed in her mind. Poison. The crippling

pain. The blood. Her hands smoothed over her abdomen and tears filled her eyes. Her child. Their child. A sob erupted from the depths of her soul. Her spirit crushed, the tears flowed freely.

Any thought of fighting disappeared like smoke on the wind. She surrendered to the overwhelming grief.

Emma and Eva worked silently to peel back the blankets. With clean, warm cloths and tender hands, they bathed her.

Through her blurred vision, she watched them wash the blood from on and between her thighs. She turned her head away in shame and sorrow. How could Francis have done this? He killed her child. He nearly killed her.

They cared for her as though she were a newborn foal and lay fresh linens beneath her to soak up any remaining blood.

Eva pursed her lips as she worked shooting irritated glances at her sister who hummed as she worked.

Ruby could not even bring herself to be ashamed at her state of undress or the unrelenting tears. The heartbreak became a constant thrumming in her chest pulsing with a life of its own. She focused on it as she stared at the canopy over the bed.

"Come now, pet. You must eat." Emma resumed her position beside the bed with a bowl in her gnarled hands.

"I have no appetite." Ruby turned away.

"No reason to force her," Eva snapped from the other side of the room. "Stubborn beast."

Ruby glared at her and gestured for the bowl. Emma offered it willingly. After a few gulps warmed her belly, Ruby pushed it aside and settled back against the bed.

Warmth and vigor from the simple meal infused her with strength. Her hands still trembled, and her legs remained useless, but if she wished to see vengeance, she needed to recover all of her strength.

Eva gathered an armful of blood-soaked linens and opened the door. The moment Emma was alone with her, Ruby seized her opportunity.

"Is there another here? A prisoner?" Ruby asked hopeful her distaste for the woman's misplaced loyalty was sufficiently concealed.

Emma spun around, her eyes wide. "I cannot say." Her voice dropped to a whisper. "He would be most displeased."

"Please," Ruby begged. "Tell me."

Emma closed her eyes and nodded.

Henry. "Is he alive?" Hope blossomed in the darkness of her soul. "I must know."

Eva reappeared. "What is this?"

"Please." Ruby's pleas rose in pitch. "Is he alive?" Tears filled her eyes again.

The stalwart sister pushed Emma aside. Her dark gaze drew Ruby in like a bottomless void, vacant of all sympathy.

"There is no knight here to save you. No one will save you. You are his." She grinned, a toothless smile full of disdain and glee. "You belong to the true king. Nothing can change that."

Eva grabbed her sister by the arm and pulled her from the room. The door slammed behind them. Ruby flinched as the lock slid into place.

The tiny blossom of hope wilted and died. Would this torment ever end? Hope faded into nothingness. Ruby followed suit, surrendering to the exhaustion, for only the nightmares offered her comfort.

Chapter Nine

On the fifth day, Crispin could no longer tolerate the strained silence drawn tight like a bowstring between himself and Ivy. His compulsion to keep her within his sights at all times intensified his intense distrust of the mysterious woman.

She pulled her cloak tighter around her shoulders and shivered. They both wore several layers in anticipation of remaining exposed to the elements for an uncertain amount of time. But even Crispin had hoped to uncover the master behind Ivy's specific orders and return to the castle within a day or two.

Ivy's gaze remained fixed on the gap in the forest overlooking the meadow. The gnarled tree reached up into the canopy of trees.

Crispin snatched the bag with their food rations and rooted around, ensuring they had enough to last them another day at least. If their quarry did not reveal themselves by the morning, they would return to the castle. He could send a small band of soldiers to keep watch over the old oak.

He sighed heavily and tossed the bag aside, leaning his head against the elm tree that served as his throne for the past few days.

"Is it empty?" Ivy's question broke the stillness. While her voice remained low, it disconcerted him to hear it after days of complete silence. Other than the occasional request to relieve herself, Ivy spoke not a word. Which suited him just perfectly. He had no intention of listening to any more of her deceptions.

"Nearly." He grunted and crossed his arms, willing the warmth to remain trapped within his heavy doublet and beneath his cloak. "If he does not appear by morning, we shall return."

"Admitting defeat?" Her mesmerizing green eyes fixed on his face with one delicate brow raised. Even after nigh on a sennight spent in the open air, hair tousled and pulling free from her braid, mud smeared across her cheek, she looked refreshed and ready for whatever may come.

"Never." Crispin scoffed. "But I cannot waste my time chasing ghosts in the forest when my queen is still missing. Unless you lied, in which case I shall take great pleasure in eviscerating you and feeding your entrails to the crows." His glare bore into her soul, and yet she did not flinch.

"He will come." Her statement rang with assurance.

Crispin regarded her silently for a long moment. How could such a woman come into the service of the Guild? What secrets she must hold in that pretty head? Rumors of the Guild floated through the kingdom for generations. They became legends, superstitions. The hooded phantasms parents used to terrify their children into compliance. In all his travels, he never met a soul connected to the Guild. At least not that he knew anyway.

Ivy's resilience impressed him. She never complained, never begged. Not so much as a whimper. The only other woman he knew with such a spirit was his Ruby. He could see how Henry would be drawn to her. Even without speaking, she carried herself with a charisma that drew attention to her without revealing her for who she truly was.

"You truly love her."

The statement pulled Crispin from his thoughts. He snorted at the ridiculousness of her observation and dropped his gaze to the old oak through the trees. Her words lingered in his mind. Of course, he loved her. His chest ached at the thought of spending another moment parted from her, wondering where she was, if she were injured, suffering...dead. He pinched his eyes closed and shook his head. There would be none of those thoughts. He banished them from his mind.

"You have never truly loved anyone but yourself." Ivy shifted against the tree and stretched her arms out, making the chain clink against her bound wrists.

"Do not speak further if you wish to keep your tongue," Crispin snapped.

"I have watched from the shadows." Ivy shrugged. "Your

behavior does not lie."

"What would a traitorous rat like you know about love?" He rounded on her unable to remain quiet. She roused a beast inside him with her mention of his affection for Ruby.

"Nothing." Her simple response lay void of all emotion.

He watched silently as she leaned back against the tree and closed her eyes. Guilt stabbed him somewhere in the vicinity of his heart. He did not trust her and with all probability, he would have her put to death for her role in these events, but he could not deny the similarity binding them. They knew nothing of love.

In truth, it terrified him. The thought of loving Ruby with this intensity. It disarmed him at moments where he could not afford to show weakness. The knowledge devastated what remained of his ego. For years he built the walls around his heart, protecting himself from the pain of rejection and heartbreak. He relied solely on himself and no one else.

Love was a dangerous emotion reserved for poets and fools. He indulged in the more pleasurable delights the world offered but never had he allowed himself the caprice of love. It brought only ruin, shame, and torment.

"Do you love him?" The question burst forth without thought. He cursed himself the moment it filled the air between them.

Her heavy exhale was the only indication she heard him. An eerie stillness settled on the hillside once more. Crispin relaxed once more thinking the conversation reached its conclusion.

"I care about him, more than anyone else. He fills my thoughts in moments of quiet. I long for his companionship. His touch." Ivy's melodic response startled him. "If that is love, then yes."

Crispin shifted uncomfortably. "Then why betray him?"

"The Guild forbids any and all attachment." Her words are spoken with such firm conviction, Crispin nearly winced at her naïve and blind obedience.

"When did you join the Guild?" Crispin asked, relenting to his curiosity.

"One does not join the Guild," Ivy spoke softly, but her

words were clear and haunting. "I was an orphan caught picking the pocket of a wealthy lord. Instead of locking me in a cell, they sold me. I was not the first. Nor the last. Children are easier to train."

Horrified, Crispin listened to her tale. His privileged life bore a poor comparison to her troubling past. He tugged at an unraveling thread on his cloak, willing himself to remain quiet and listen.

"I attempted to escape the first night in their care. They beat me until I could not walk, then chained me in a dungeon until I vowed to obey." Her calm tone lay in stark contrast to the ominous words. "They trained me. As a thief, a spy, an assassin—whatever they required, I was obligated to obey my master. When I finished my training, I was sold."

"To whom?" Crispin dared to break the flow of her tale.

"My master." Ivy's glassy eyes met his. "I must submit without question until my duty is fulfilled and my master releases me from my bond."

An icy dread settled around him. He shivered against the unexpected chill. The terrifying tales he heard about the Guild could not begin to compare to Ivy's recounting. She suffered at the hands of the Guild, this much was certain. Was it possible to save someone so entrenched in something so evil?

Crispin swallowed hard. They had been gone too long. With this new information, he knew he would be unable to face this unknown foe without someone to fight alongside him. Ivy could be a liability.

He quietly gathered their items and rose to his feet. As he worked packing the gear, Ivy watched him. When her attention shifted to the meadow below, Crispin stilled.

"He has come." Her reverent words made his skin prickle.

A glance confirmed the presence of a horse and rider entering the meadow.

"Shit." Crispin grabbed the rag and gagged Ivy before ensuring she remained securely bound to the tree. She offered no resistance.

The sun dipped below the horizon, casting long shadows

through the already hazy twilight. Crispin pulled up his hood and drew the dagger from his belt sheath. He carefully wove down the hill through the trees to the narrow entrance of the meadow.

His gaze skimmed the trees nearby. It seemed the rider arrived alone, which bode well for his ability to subdue the man. A horse grazed in the tall grass. Crispin moved with stealth to not spook the animal.

The rider knelt before the tree, a deep hood pulled over his head. Judging from the breadth of their shoulders, it could not be a woman. The man reached into the same hole where Ivy left the message several days prior. As he removed the leather pouch, Crispin seized his opportunity and rushed forward with his weapon at the ready.

With a cry, he tackled the rider to the ground and pinned him down. His body went limp beneath the pressure of Crispin atop him. In the encroaching darkness, Crispin could not make out the face of his enemy. He pressed the blade to the man's throat.

"Who are you?" His demand rang through the small glen, making the horse sidestep with agitation.

"Flee. Quickly." The ominous warning came from a familiar voice.

"Henry?" Crispin dropped the blade and ripped the hood from the man's head. In the dying twilight, Henry's battered visage filled Crispin with equal measures of hope and horror.

"What did you say?" He shook Henry, but the man lay limp against the thick grass. He leaned close, feeling Henry's breath on his cheek, and sighed in relief. He was not dead. But judging from the bruises and swollen, bloody eye, he soon would be if the wounds were not treated with haste.

"Henry." Crispin shook him. "Wake up." Nothing roused him. *Shit.*

Somehow he needed to get Henry back to the castle. Perhaps he could appeal to Ivy's softer nature. She confessed her affinity for Henry. If she saw him in such a state, surely she would come to his aid. He could not tend to an injured man and mind a prisoner simultaneously. He swore and raked his hand through his hair.

Message forgotten, Crispin slowly rose and retrieved the horse from the other side of the meadow. He tied the reins to a twisted branch of the old oak. With all the strength he could muster, he lifted Henry. He staggered under the weight of his friend and clung tighter, willing himself to hold steady.

With agonizing steps, Crispin made his way to the horse and managed to pull Henry across the saddle. He leaned against the horse's neck and took several deep breaths. How the hell was Henry so damned heavy?

After ensuring his friend was secure, he untied the horse and led it out of the meadow. Darkness had fully descended on the forest. Crispin swore. Even if they left now, 'twould be damned near impossible to weave through the thick brush and trees and reached a passable road.

Henry needed a healer. Even if he attempted to reach Marian's cottage, the same issues would hinder their progress sacrificing valuable time fumbling around in the darkness. He slowly led the horse up the hill to where he and Ivy had sat in wait.

Only the spot where he tied Ivy to the tree lay vacant. There was no sign of his prisoner.

"God's blood, teeth, and bones!" Crispin swore, spinning around. Panic suffused him, causing his blood to race. How in the devil had she escaped?

He searched for Ghost, who had been tethered nearby, but there was no glimpse of his glossy gray coat in the rising moonlight. Resigned, Crispin tied the horse Henry had ridden to a nearby tree and gathered whatever supplies remained scattered on the ground.

Leaving her unattended had been a rash move on his part. He should have known better than to trust she would remain compliant. She warned him. Her loyalty belonged to her master. Crispin spat on the ground and draped the bags over the back of the saddle beside Henry.

He freed the horse and slowly made his way down the hill once more with painfully slow steps. Of all moments to appear,

Henry chose twilight. He shook his head as they ventured away from the hidden meadow.

As he walked, Crispin's mind churned. He came to a stop when the realization doused him with a cold touch of dread. Henry arrived in the meadow. He knew where to find the message. His family had a hand in the raid designed to kill Ruby as a child.

Crispin stumbled back and rested his hand against the horse's neck. He glanced at the unconscious body of his friend draped over the saddle. Surely he could not be the master she spoke of. He shook the rancid thoughts from his mind. There was no proof of Henry's treachery. He had been a faithful friend and ally for years.

Unless Ivy poisoned him against Crispin, using him for her own twisted plot. His head ached from the horrid thoughts swirling in the depths of his mind. He pushed them aside. First, he would find a place to rest and revive Henry. Then he would confront him.

Pushing forward, Crispin ignored everything but the determination to reach the main road and locate shelter for the night.

The soft song of a nightingale in the trees echoed the call of an owl. Crispin forged onward, his mind bound in torment. He was no closer to finding Ruby than he had been before, and his prisoner had escaped, but at least he recovered Henry.

After wandering the thick woods well into the night, they spilled out onto the king's road. With the moon high above them, he led the way in the direction of the nearest village.

Thunder echoed in the distance. Crispin swore and walked faster wishing he had Ghost to carry him.

The thunder grew louder making Crispin turn. He blinked in disbelief at the blur of gray racing toward him. Was that Ghost? Before he could draw his sword, the incoming horse knocked him backward. He stumbled, slamming into the horse carrying Henry. The horse squealed and sidestepped causing Crispin to lose his balance and fall to the ground.

Scrambling to right himself, Crispin struggled to pull the

sword from his scabbard. Shadows played in the scattered moonlight.

"Show yourself!" He braced himself for the oncoming fight, but nothing prepared him for the pain shooting through his skull as his assailant struck his head from behind.

Crispin collapsed against the dirt and the world around him disappeared as he joined Henry in the land of dreams and nightmares.

Chapter Ten

The gentle rocking did nothing to improve the pounding in his head. Henry wrenched his eyes open. Darkness. He blinked a few times, wondering if somehow he lost his vision. The flicker of movement below told him he still possessed those faculties, even with his one eye still swollen.

Hooves. Dirt. Intense pressure against his chest. It took a few moments to realize he was draped over the back of a horse. The memories slowly filtered into his mind. Riding to the meadow. The twisted oak tree. A message hidden inside. He twisted his head but recognized none of the surroundings thanks to the darkness. Even the moonlight helped little, thanks to the thick clouds blocking its glow.

Henry shifted his weight, but his arms lay weak beside him. He tugged but to no avail. They were bound tightly. He swore beneath his breath and pinched his eyes closed to fight off the wave of sickness from the motion of the horse.

In an effort to ignore the rebellious twisting in his gut, he focused his thoughts instead on how he came to be in such an uncomfortable situation. Francis gave him little recourse, threatening to torture Ruby unless he complied with his demands.

The two guards led him blindfolded from the cell. They put him on a horse and led him from whatever fortress Francis occupied. The solid thud of hooves on stone shifted to softer terrain. They passed rushing water. A river or stream perhaps. He could not tell the hour or the direction in which they traveled. He swayed in the saddle, his bound hands gripping the horse's mane to keep from falling off.

When they had reached their destination, the guards removed his blindfold and gave him explicit directions. Follow the trail to the hidden meadow. Retrieve the message within the oak tree. Return post haste. If he did not follow these directions, Ruby would suffer the consequences of his failure.

He failed her once before. He would not do so again.

With difficulty, he urged the horse to follow the narrow trail. The sun set in the distance, making the entrance difficult to find. But the meadow was where they said it would be. The tree contained a small satchel. He put it in his pocket and then...he was ambushed.

Crispin. He groaned when the memory revealed itself like a flash of lightning. He tried to warn him and then nothing. Days without food and care left him weak and exhausted. He could not fight back. Could not warn his friend.

Henry glanced ahead noting the familiar horse, leading the one which carried him. Crispin lay draped across the saddle in the same manner. A hooded figure led Ghost by the reins.

He relaxed again, allowing his head to hang. Such strain drained him of whatever strength remained. He breathed in and out, over and over, until he could focus on nothing but the journey. The sound of rushing water returned. When the cadence of the horse's steps echoed on the hard cobblestone, Henry bristled.

They were being returned to Francis.

Whoever wore the hood must be in Francis's employ. He wished for nothing more than to run a blade through the back of the traitorous bastard who dared align himself with such a deviant snake.

Henry restrained his immediate impulse to break free and fight. They were bound, and in his weakened state, resistance would serve no purpose other than to sustain more injury. Instead, Henry feigned unconsciousness. When the horse came to a halt, Henry braced himself for the incoming assault.

"You have done well." Francis's voice grated against Henry's throbbing skull.

Henry could no longer pretend when a firm hand ripped him from the saddle and tossed him to the ground. He groaned and rolled onto his side, glaring up at the bastard he once called a friend.

Francis stood in the middle of a well-lit courtyard with a twisted smile of joy on his withered lips. "Still alive, I see. How delightful."

Crispin landed in a heap beside him. The impact shook him awake. He struggled against his bonds for a moment before he met Henry's gaze. Then, as if sensing his brother's presence, he turned to face Francis.

"You wretched son of a bitch." Crispin attempted to scramble to his feet and charge at Francis, but the two guards rushed forward and beat him into compliance.

Henry's gut twisted in sympathy at the sight of Crispin doubled over, his head pressed to the stone as he caught his breath. When he lifted his head, he spat a mouthful of blood before meeting Francis's gaze once more.

"Mark my words, brother, I will strip you of your dignity before I end your life. This I vow." Crispin's words made the hair on Henry's neck stand on end. If there were ever a soul one should never cross, 'twas Crispin. Francis would be wise to take this warning to heart.

Their captor, however, seemed unperturbed by Crispin's outburst.

A gentle rhythmic tapping came from behind him. He turned to see the hooded figure watching the proceeding reunion like a specter. For a moment, Henry forgot about the traitor who sold them.

"Traitorous bitch. I was right to not trust you." Crispin glowered. "I should have run you through when I had the opportunity."

Confusion shrouded Henry's mind. Who was this? Before he could speak, their captor peeled back his hood. An icy blade pierced Henry's soul.

"Ivy." He murmured her name with equal measures of horror and reverence. His heart split at the sight of her lovely face and those wide eyes, green as a spring meadow.

"I have done as you commanded." Ivy's voice sent another wave of spasms through Henry's broken body. She ignored him and focused solely on Francis. "Release me from my obligation."

"Why would I release my most valuable asset?" Francis studied her carefully.

Ivy stiffened but remained silent.

"With you by my side, I would be unstoppable. Such a lethal beauty would ensure my transition is completed without any further—delays." He cocked his head and smiled.

"I have fulfilled my obligations. Release me," Ivy repeated. Even though she attempted to maintain an impassive tone, Henry heard the waver of emotion beneath the surface. He hated himself for caring even though she betrayed them, repeatedly and without remorse.

"Very well." Francis reached beneath his cloak and pulled a small roll of parchment into view. He held it out in one gloved hand, and when she stepped forward to take it, he withdrew. "First, we should celebrate. Go inside. My servants will tend you. You deserve a reprieve and a hot meal before you take your leave. 'Tis the least I can do for your dedicated service."

Ivy's hands clenched into fists, but she nodded and pushed past him to enter the towering building behind Francis.

Henry saw the current of tension between them. He never imagined Ivy would have been taking directions from Francis. He cursed himself for allowing her to manipulate him so effectively. He should have taken her to Crispin when he had the opportunity. Once again, he failed and there was naught he could do to alter their fate.

"Members of the Guild are not known for their loyalty." Crispin rose against his brother.

"What would you know of loyalty?" Francis scoffed, dropping all pretenses and revealing the wicked side Crispin tried to warn them about when they uncovered the monk's true identity. "I paid well enough for her loyalty. Without her, I would never have been able to seize the perfect moment and take the one thing you value more than yourself."

Henry sat silently watching the interaction between the brothers. He swayed still bound and weak. Seeing Ivy, knowing she betrayed him yet again, struck a painful blow. He almost wished she would have killed him and left him in the forest. Save him the agony of such a revelation. Crispin's response drew him from his poisoned thoughts.

"Where is she?" Crispin slowly rose to his feet. The guards stepped forward, their blades drawn and ready. Crispin ignored them. Even bound and hobbled, he commanded respect in his stance.

The brothers locked in a silent battle of wills. Henry wished he had all his faculties in order to join the inevitable fight lying on the horizon. He hung on the tension, waiting for the moment one of them would break.

"Where is Ruby?" Crispin repeated. His eyes blazed like a vicious internal inferno.

"She is quite safe, I assure you." Francis crossed his arms.

"I demand to see her." Crispin took a step closer bringing the tip of one of the guard's blades against his doublet. "Without delay."

"You are in no position to give orders." Francis held steady, his infuriating confidence burrowed beneath Henry's skin. "Within these walls, I am king. Soon, the whole of Meradin will also agree. Your time has come to an end, and I will take my rightful place."

A vengeful scream wrenched from Crispin's throat. He attempted to lunge for Francis. But the guards intercepted without hesitation. They threw Crispin to the ground and pinned him against the stone with boots and blades.

Henry watched helpless as they beat him into submission with their fists and the pommels of their swords. Their blows driving into Crispin's torso and head repeatedly. He closed his eyes unable to watch any longer.

"Enough." Francis's command silenced the commotion, leaving Crispin's echoing groans of pain to fill the silence. "Take them both to the dungeon."

Two of the guards lifted Crispin between them. Another guard came behind Henry and jerked him to his feet. He followed the men carrying Crispin being mindful to keep his gaze lowered. They entered a door on the side of the tower and wove down the staircase.

Henry marked the distance between the door and the dungeon. A small keep, weakly fortified. He had enough sense to tuck these details into the back of his mind. They would be useful should the opportunity for escape arise. He counted a dozen men, perhaps more.

The guards tossed Crispin onto the floor of the cell then threw Henry in beside him. The cell was narrow and dark. Henry shuddered at the memory of being locked inside it without food or water. It became impossible to breathe.

He clawed at his throat and rushed for the door. The guard slammed it in his face. His laughter echoed down the corridor beyond. Henry slammed his fists against the wood.

Weakness pulled him down to the floor. He leaned his head against the door and surrendered to the obvious. Francis would never allow them to live. Death would come for them both, of that he was sure.

Chapter Eleven

Ruby loathed the two women designated as her jailers. Eva proved to be worse than Emma, but both women were loyal to Francis. Nothing could dissuade them from their blind obedience.

When they woke her at dawn, Ruby begrudgingly allowed them to care for her. If only because they arrived with a sturdy tub and began to fill it with steaming water. She longed for a bath to soothe her aching body and revitalize her soul.

The sweet scent of rosemary filled the air. Ruby twisted in the bed to watch the slow progress as they filled the tub. Her gaze lingered longingly on the open door. She shifted slowly to a sitting position, ignoring the protests of her heavy limbs and aching body.

Emma appeared before her. "Best not move too quickly, pet. You are still weak as a kitten."

Ruby ripped her arm from beneath the woman's touch. "Only because you allowed him to poison me." She could not keep the venom from her voice as the grief settled around her heart once more. No amount of time or rest would banish the searing ache. Even in the midst of her pain, she would not allow Francis to gloat in his success. She would fight him until her dying breath.

The old woman drew back, her eyes filled with hurt. Ruby could not find any conscience in her actions. These women were sent to prepare her for Francis. They were his loyal servants, and no amount of pleading or begging would convince them to free her.

Eva watched the interaction from the opposite side of the room where she poured scented oil and herbs into the steaming water. Although the women looked similar in stature and coloring, there was a distinct difference in their posture and expression. Ruby saw the resentment in Eva's dark eyes. Emma's kind gestures reflected a more tender nature.

It mattered not for they were not her friends nor allies. They were in the service of her enemy, and she would give them no consideration when she fully regained her strength.

Ruby struggled to rise to her feet, gripping the bedpost with both hands. Emma stood nearby, ready to lend her assistance. She swatted the woman's hands away twice before she was able to fully put her weight on her feet. Even in her state of complete undress, Ruby could not muster the strength to feel shame. Francis, these women, and every miserable soul in his service could strip her of every shred of clothing and decency, but they would not steal her spirit.

The cold air from the corridor crept over her skin, making her shiver. She stared longingly at the steaming bath.

Emma offered her hand. "Come. Let me help you."

"I would rather freeze to death than let you touch me again." Ruby glared at the woman.

"Stubborn wench," Eva muttered as she passed by to fetch the linens from the servant lingering by the door.

Emma backed away and busied herself with tidying the bed.

Ruby grimaced at the bloodstains on the bed linens and turned away. It would do her no good to dwell upon it. She could grieve in her own time, but her survival lay in her recovery. One step at a time.

With great effort, she released the bedpost and took a long moment to find her balance. Pride filled her at the accomplishment. Her legs wobbled as she took a tentative step toward the bath. Then another. She put her arms out to balance, reaching for the tub as she made slow progress.

When she reached her goal, her heart nearly burst. Such a small victory, but for the first time in ages, Ruby felt hopeful. She gripped the side of the tub and slowly stepped into the steaming water.

The scent of rosemary and lavender brought memories of home to the forefront of her mind like the reflective surface of a lake. She lowered herself into the water and sighed with contentment as the warmth sank beneath her skin.

Her hands skimmed over her arms and legs under the water. The bruises had faded from purple to yellow. The heat of the water eased any lingering soreness. She retrieved the cloth from the edge of the tub and dipped it in the water. Running it over her shoulders and chest, Ruby savored the rasp of the cloth on her skin scrubbing the events of the past several days from her exhausted body.

Emma busied herself with the linens on the bed while Eva retrieved garments from the tall wardrobe in the corner.

While remaining aware of their presence, Ruby tried not to dwell on them instead focusing on absorbing the restorative properties of the herbal bath. Her mother would have encouraged her to add some calendula and dandelion.

The mere thought of her mother brought tears to her eyes. She swiped them away before they could manifest fully. This would not be the end. She would see her mother again. And Crispin. A stirring persistence settled around her heart.

Ruby bathed in silence. She protested only briefly when Emma offered to wash her hair. Lifting her arms to do so herself proved too exhausting at the moment, so she relented.

Emma used fresh water to rinse the soap from her hair. She used scented oils to loosen any remaining tangles before rinsing it again.

Ruby's hand rested over her swollen stomach. A tear slipped free at the thought of the life no longer growing inside her. She allowed herself a silent moment of contemplation while Emma finished her ministrations.

"Come, pet, before the water grows cold." The old woman nudged her shoulder.

With trembling hands, Ruby gripped the side of the tub and lifted herself from the water. A fire burned in the hearth, but it did nothing to stop the chill from sinking into her the moment she left the warm embrace of the water. She shivered, and Emma rushed forward with clean linens to dry her.

Exhausted, Ruby decided not to fight against the woman's

aid. Her gaze fell on the bed where a lovely kirtle and overskirt lay waiting. The rich hues of scarlet and blue were interlaced with gold stitching. She recognized the colors Francis chose for his own doublet and shivered again, but this time it was not from the cold.

"Worry not. All will be well, pet." Emma's poor attempt to soothe her intensified the foreboding air gathering around the keep like an impending storm.

With both women working to draw the clean garments over her head, the process took very little time. As much as she detested the idea of wearing his colors, the clothes provided warmth and modesty. Two things she valued with an acute awareness after Francis stole her from her sanctuary.

Eva instructed the servants to remove the bath and retreated with the soiled linens while Emma led Ruby to a seat beside the fire. With firm but gentle strokes, she brushed her hair, allowing it to dry as she worked.

The rhythmic ministrations lulled her into a peaceful repose. After a few minutes, Ruby could no longer remain silent.

"Why go to this trouble?" Ruby asked the woman braiding her hair.

"My lord wishes for you to join him. He has a gift for you."

Fear clutched her throat and squeezed. A gift. Ruby wished for nothing from him but her freedom as well as Henry's. There could be nothing he could possibly offer that would heal the wound he caused and allowed to fester into a seething hatred. He could draw his own blade across his throat and it would not sate her need for vengeance. The only gift he could bestow upon her that would bring her joy would be his slow, painful, agonizing death and disintegration into obscurity.

A gift from Francis would bring her no joy, of that she was certain.

Emma finished braiding her hair and pinning it into place. Eva returned and set a pair of leather slippers on the floor at Ruby's feet.

"He demands your presence." Eva sniffed with indignance and stepped aside. "Come along."

Ruby rose from her seat slowly. Once she found her balance, she squared her shoulders and took a bold step. She would face him, but she would not bow to him. One thing she would never do again was underestimate Francis. He might have played the part of a pious monk, but he was nothing short of a wicked incarnation of evil sent to plague Meradin.

What she knew of his reputation before the fire played at odds with the man who now held her captive. Almost as though his soul spit between darkness and light allowing the dark to consume him completely. Nothing about his radical transformation made any logical sense. He played them all for fools, and now they suffered the consequences of their ignorance.

By the time she reached the door, Ruby found an inner reserve of fortitude. Every step brought her courage and determination. She would face him on her own terms.

Henry would not save her. Neither would Crispin. If she wished to survive and defeat Francis, she would need to save herself. She would bide her time and her strength until he revealed his weakness. Then she would strike.

In the corridor, Eva led the way while Emma followed behind flanked by two guards. Ruby ignored the prickling of awareness as their gazes lingered on her. She focused on her even steps and maintaining her balance as they descended the narrow staircase.

At the base of the stairs, they turned right into a wide hall leading to an oversized wooden door. Francis waited behind it. There was no question in her mind. He summoned her, and this was merely his way of intimidating her into compliance.

There was nothing he could do to her that he had not already done. He refused to kill her. What could possibly be a fate worse than death? Death would be a welcome release, but she would not give him the satisfaction of bringing her misery. Whatever waited beyond those doors, she would endure with the same strength she possessed through the entirety of this ordeal.

With a deep breath, Ruby paused outside the doors. The guards came forward and opened them. Inside the cavernous room, Francis sat upon a large carved mahogany throne. His gaze consumed her as she entered the room.

"My queen." He rose from his seat and stepped down from the raised dais.

Ruby held her tongue and stopped in the center of the room refusing to bow to her captor.

"You have done well," he complimented the two older women who bowed low in his presence. "Leave us." He dismissed them with a wave of his hand.

The sisters retreated, leaving Francis alone with her and the two guards attending the door.

"I see you are recovering well." Francis paced around her. He traced his fingers over her shoulder.

Ruby flinched at the touch and glared at him. "Why have you summoned me?"

"Must you be so ungrateful?" Francis tutted with disappointment. "I have a gift for you, my sweet."

"There is nothing you could give me that will ensure my compliance and loyalty." Ruby recoiled when he lifted his hand, anticipating his wrath.

"Bring them in." He addressed the guards and dropped his hands, clasping them behind his back as he retreated.

Confused, Ruby spun around to face the door when it burst open. Two guards appeared carrying a man between them. *Henry.* Another pair of men entered just behind him bearing another prisoner. *Crispin.*

A gasp burst from her lips at the sight of the man she loved hanging limp between the two guards. Whatever hope she bolstered within herself withered at the sight of them in chains. She watched in horror as the guards dumped the two men on the floor at her feet and withdrew.

Ruby dropped to her knees beside Crispin's limp body. He was breathing, but blood smeared across his face and clothes. She reached for Henry and found him in much the same condition but with abrasions across his face and a swollen, blackened eye. Henry groaned at her touch but did not wake.

"What have you done to them?" Ruby rounded on Francis

who seemed amused by her tender concern for the wounded prisoners.

"Nothing less than they deserved." Francis motioned to the guards again who appeared carrying wooden buckets. "Wake them."

Ruby scrambled back as the guards doused the two unconscious men with cold water. They shifted and groaned, waking from the unnatural slumber in a haze. She watched helpless as they shook the liquid from their eyes and searched their surroundings.

Crispin met her gaze. "Ruby." Relief filled his hoarse voice. He struggled to rise, nearly falling over twice before he was able to find his footing and brace himself with his bound hands.

Henry rolled to his side, but he slumped back against the ground, weak and exhausted.

Ruby longed to rush to his side and offer aid, but Francis gripped her arm when she took a step toward Henry and Crispin.

A vengeful cloud settled on Crispin's countenance. "Get your hand off my queen."

"You are in no position to offer demands, brother." Francis laughed, and the chilling sound echoed in the imposter's throne room.

The murderous glare in Crispin's eyes should have offered her comfort, but it did nothing but instill fear. If she learned anything about Francis, she knew there was a larger game at play. She steeled herself knowing Francis would make this next move as painful as possible.

Chapter Twelve

Rage and relief consumed him simultaneously. Ruby stood before him clad in his brother's decadent colors. The gentle curves of her face lay gaunt and shadowed, haunted by events he could not possibly attempt to understand. The desire to reach for her compelled him.

Holding her gaze, he stepped forward. The chains binding his hands rattled and pulled tight as he reached for her.

Francis pulled her closer. She flinched at his touch, turning her face away from him in disgust.

"I will not tell you again." Crispin demanded, "Release her."

The rising tide inside pushed him closer to action. He cursed his bonds and longed for the firm grip of his sword. His gaze lingered on Francis's hand where it rested on Ruby's arm. He wanted nothing more than to separate it permanently from his person. Just the knowledge of what terror his brother must have wrought upon her to wipe the brilliance from her smile and the light from her eyes left him engulfed in fury.

"*My* queen is precisely where she belongs." Francis's mangled smile and the flash of determination in his blue eyes infuriated Crispin further. Ruby trembled beside him.

Crispin waited until her gaze met his once more. She tipped her chin up, but he did not miss the silent tears staining her cheeks. His once valiant warrior queen stood battered and bruised before him, yet she refused to break. He took hope in this small gesture. The desire to take her into his arms nearly brought him to his knees. But he would not concede defeat to Francis, not while a breath remained in his body.

"What have you done to her?" He redirected his ire toward the man responsible for their suffering.

"I have restored balance. Purged the wicked seed growing inside her and prepared her to take her rightful place beside me."

Francis's response echoed with confidence and pride.

The implication of his words nearly passed by unnoticed. Crispin bristled as the meaning took root in his mind.

Ruby's hand moved to cover the lower part of her stomach, where their child grew inside her. Her gaze slipped away from his, and the tears fell freely, dripping onto the floor. She swiped them away. Francis held her tight beside him.

"You bastard!" Crispin loosed the fury inside him. He bolted forward uncaring of the chains or the guards surrounding him. He stopped short of his brother's reach when the cold press of two blades touched his throat. A warm trickle of blood ran down his chest beneath his garments. He ignored the pain and temporary discomfort. There would be vengeance for Francis's unspeakable betrayals.

"Give me an excuse to kill you. I beg you." Francis grinned. "'Twould make my claim even stronger." He studied Crispin with unbridled pleasure.

"Forgive me, my liege. I failed to protect them." Henry's broken voice echoed behind him.

Crispin could not bear to look at his companion or his bride. The anguish proved too much. Instead, he focused solely on the man responsible for the destruction of everything he held sacred. He imagined driving a blade straight through his brother's heart, watching the life drain from his eyes and bathing in the satisfaction of ridding the world of his tainted soul.

"On my honor, I will rip your heart from your chest as atonement for what you have done," Crispin growled, allowing the darkness to pulse through him. "You are no longer the honorable man I once knew if you ever truly were." He watched the amusement fade from Francis's scarred visage. "What evil must have tarnished your soul to the point you would kill an innocent, savage your own blood, and steal what you do not deserve?"

Francis pressed his lips together and cocked his head in contemplation. "What difference is my quest from your own? Have kings not utilized such methods for centuries, garnering empires beyond imagination? Who am I to deny my birthright and shun the same methods which have ensured the survival of my ancestors for generations?"

Crispin could not argue with his logic, no matter how flawed and brutal it seemed. Bloodshed and betrayal littered the battlefields and ruins of empires dating back to the beginning of time. He held his brother's gaze.

"Why did you not come forward years ago? Father would have welcomed you with open arms." Crispin scoffed. "His golden child returned from the dead."

"My recovery prevented my return. Life proceeded as though I never existed, but this time spent in waiting brought me invaluable insights and led me down the path I was meant to follow." A wicked smile claimed Francis's lips. "Watching your decline into disgrace proved far too entertaining. You played your role to perfection. A fallen prince hellbent on hedonism and drowning in self-indulgence. I could not have planned it better myself."

Crispin recoiled more at the statement than the twisted visage before him.

"I watched as you brought yourself ruin. You alone proved yourself unfit to be ruler of Meradin. Even Father recognized your inability to rise to his high standards and fill the role I left vacant." Francis's cold laugh made his blood chill. "Is that why you killed him?"

Ruby gasped. A muttered curse came from Henry. Crispin refused to react. Francis was baiting him, leading him to confess. He focused solely on the lying bastard and narrowed his gaze.

"I did not kill him." Crispin embraced the silence following his declaration.

Francis tutted and released Ruby who stumbled away from both of them, bracing herself against the wall. "Come now. You may not have killed him with your own blade, but 'twas your impetuous order that sealed his fate."

Crispin pursed his lips, refusing to allow Francis to poison the minds of the two people he held most dear in this world. If he lost them, he would have nothing. His will to live would dissipate if he allowed this vicious rumor to take root.

Francis paced the floor, daring to come closer. He leaned forward, as though sharing a secret between them, his voice low and measured. Crispin jerked the chains, but the guards remained steadfast, their blades poised to kill with a simple order.

"I know of your clandestine meeting. The hooded assassin outside the tavern." Francis's breath reeked of ale, his eyes glowed with an unholy flame.

Without a flicker of emotion, Crispin remained steadfast as a marble statue. Inside, his mind rioted. How in the devil did Francis know about that meeting? 'Twas never meant to proceed. He had been drunk, angry, and bitter. There had been no details shared, no agreement made. But Crispin had paid him. He clenched his teeth to keep from reacting and betraying his guilt.

"I see you cannot deny your involvement in the plot." Francis circled him. "No matter. You condemn yourself with your silence."

A hundred thoughts flashed through Crispin's mind. Yet he could not grasp one that would serve him well. He remained still and focused on the ornately carved chair at the head of the room. The one Francis used as his makeshift throne. He inhaled deep, steeling himself for the assault on his character.

Francis was not wrong. He was a selfish bastard with no direction and no loyalty. He hated his father and his brother. For years they refused to see his strengths and encourage them. He clung to whatever afforded him comfort and pleasure, rejecting the presumptuous designs of his bloodline. Upon Francis's death, Crispin took heart in the knowledge the throne would one day be his until his father ripped his birthright from him and threatened to present it to someone even less deserving.

His behavior had been rash and foolish, but in the end, he could not endure his mother's censure should she discover his involvement in the king's death. Even after his father banished him, he sent word to the hooded assassin. Keep the gold, but forgo the orders.

To this day, he never truly knew whether it was his order which sealed his father's fate. That knowledge haunted him.

"You brought ruin upon yourself, brother." Francis stopped pacing.

Crispin met his gaze, hoping the hatred would be evident without words.

"All I had to do was wait and allow you to destroy your own reputation. Then I reappear, miraculously spared by the horrible fire, but not untouched by its devastation, the people of Meradin will see the rightful heir restored to the throne destined to save the kingdom from chaos and ruin." Francis laughed.

"Burn in hell," Crispin spat, his patience wearing with every passing moment. "You son of a bitch."

"Such a temper in a king is unacceptable." Francis pointed a gloved hand at him. "This prison is of your own making. I can only thank you for reuniting me with my betrothed. While I knew of her value before she became entangled in your web of seduction, I could never have imagined the good fortune of recovering the lost jewel of England."

He glanced at Ruby who braced herself against the wall. Those luminous eyes intoxicated him still. Fate brought them together. She saved him. Brought him back from the brink of his destruction. He loved her deeply before he knew of her heritage. She would belong to him alone until the end of time.

Undeterred by Francis's threats, he declared his love with a simple look. The tension around her mouth softened.

"Take one final look, Crispin. She belongs to me, and you will finally get what you deserve."

I love you. Ruby mouthed the words as tears spilled free.

Crispin nodded, unable to form the words himself as the guards seized him by the arms and dragged him from the room.

Ruby's shouts of protest echoed down the corridor.

He barely glimpsed the other guards dragging Henry from the chamber behind them. They carried him down the stairs leading to the dungeon. Crispin fought against their hold, but they held him fast, releasing him only when they tossed both him and Henry onto the cold, damp stone floor of the prison cell.

The door slammed behind them.

Crispin shouted, banging his fists on the wooden door,

dredging up every curse he could muster from the depths of his tormented soul. The sound of a second door slamming only redoubled his efforts.

A scream echoing from somewhere overhead sent a bolt of dread straight to the pit of his stomach. *Ruby.*

He bowed his head against the door and prayed, unsure if anyone would hear his plea. *Be strong, my love. I will come for you.*

Chapter Thirteen

Fighting against the pain, Henry dragged himself up to sit on the narrow bed. Crispin's shouts reverberated off the walls. Icy tendrils of fear seized his heart at the sound of Ruby's distant scream. Crispin pounded his fists against the door, cursing and shouting until he grew hoarse.

Henry could offer no comfort. In truth, he was drained. There was no physical strength left in him. No matter how much his mind and soul raged against the injustice of their imprisonment and their treatment within Francis's small fortress.

As Crispin raged, Henry watched in stunned silence. He braced himself for the inevitable moment looming on the horizon where his friend would turn and unleash his ire upon him. Blame him for allowing them to be captured, for not protecting Ruby. For leading him into a trap. For allowing himself to be seduced by a traitor and manipulated by his own blood kin. Crispin had every right to punish him for his failures. He would take responsibility for his actions and bear the consequences.

Henry leaned back against the wall, prepared to take the full force of Crispin's fury. His good eye focused on his friend and king. Crispin stilled, his fists and head pressed against the door.

The helplessness hovering out of reach for the past few days finally settled upon Henry's weary shoulders. Seeing Crispin's response to Francis's confession and hearing the horrors Ruby endured at the hands of such a heartless villain left him despondent. He licked his lips and groaned when he shifted his weight unsettled by the sudden shift in Crispin's demeanor. Henry could no longer bear the tension.

"My most profound apologies, sire. I have not only failed you but the queen." Tears filled his eyes. "I could not protect her." A sob lodged in his throat. He mumbled beneath his breath, apologizing repeatedly until his words became a litany begging for forgiveness.

Crispin remained against the door, his face hidden away. The silence descended like a shroud smothering what remained of Henry's composure. His shoulders trembled as the tears fell. All restraint turned to ash when Henry allowed the emotions to overwhelm him.

"Forgive me," he muttered. "I beg you." His voice echoed in the cell, casting an almost reverent air upon the room like a priest raising his hands to the heavens begging for salvation from his sinful ways.

Henry hung his head. Even Crispin had forsaken him. His failures earned him the scorn of the one man he loved and honored more than his brothers. He would bear the sins upon himself into the next life. There was no salvation for a man such as him. A disappointment to all those who entrusted their safety to his care.

A soft touch on his shoulder made Henry flinch. He lifted his gaze to find Crispin staring down at him. No scorn lay in his eyes. No admonishment. No revulsion. Henry swallowed hard and quelled his tears.

"There is nothing we can do for the past." Crispin's voice cracked, strained from shouting through the door demanding Ruby's release. "I know where your loyalty lies. You fought valiantly. There is no shame in acknowledging defeat."

Henry blinked at Crispin in disbelief. Could this possibly be the same man with whom he spent over half his life in service to? Never before had Crispin shown such a side of himself. For years, Crispin bore the titles of self-indulgent and unrepentant with pride. But hearing him embrace the mistakes of his past and learn from them seemed quite out of place.

"Are you injured, sire? Your head, I mean?" Henry stiffened when Crispin sat on the bed beside him.

"My head feels as though a pike has been run through it, but I am in full possession of my faculties." Crispin let his gaze wander the cell. There was nothing in the room save them. Not even a pot to piss in. He returned his gaze to Henry. "What happened the night they took you?"

Relaxing against the wall once more, Henry recounted his tale to the best of his ability. Some of the details were clouded and weak, but he faithfully relayed as much as he could remember. Crispin sat in silence with his lips pursed. His blue eyes darkened like a storm-filled summer sky. When he finished telling him of their orders for him to retrieve the message in the hidden meadow, his voice trailed off. Crispin knew the rest.

"When did you uncover Ivy's duplicity?" Crispin rounded on him, the question throwing him off balance.

"The day after I brought Francis to the castle." Henry dropped his gaze, filling with shame once more. "I found her leaving your presence chamber. Later, I uncovered an item she stole from your possession. A piece of parchment written in French bearing the royal seal."

Crispin growled, but he maintained his composure. "Why did you not come to me when you discovered her?"

"I care for her." His chest tightened at the confession. "I knew if I brought her to you with this accusation, you would try her for treason or worse, execute her without a second thought." Henry shook his head. "I could not bear to see her die."

"Why did you release her?" Crispin's deceptively calm response terrified Henry.

"I did not release her." Henry clenched his fists in the thin blanket beneath him. "I locked her in the north tower. I questioned her nightly. I begged her to reveal the details of who sent her. Offered clemency in exchange for a name, anything. Something in exchange for her safety."

"And did she concede?"

"She refused, claiming she was a member of the Guild and could not break their code or her contract with her master." Henry's memory drifted to those nights tucked in the north tower when he attempted to convince her of his sincerity, of his commitment to saving her. Her betrayal stung. Not once, but twice he found himself at the mercy of her scheming treachery. Even so, whatever tendre he held for her could not be denied, no matter how he wished to relinquish it.

'Twas obvious she felt nothing for him. Her dual betrayal spoke more clearly than words ever could. With such a lovely face and tempting figure, she proved too enticing for him to ignore. How he wished he could forget the delightful release she brought him, the lusty moments spent entwined in a passionate embrace. The woman was poison sent to destroy Meradin by bringing ruin to Henry and Crispin, plunging the kingdom into chaos.

"You were able to persuade her to reveal so much." Crispin studied him for a long moment. "But you chose to release her instead of bringing her before me to receive the justice she deserved?"

"I never released her, sire," Henry confessed honestly. "While 'tis true I kept her hidden and concealed her treasonous actions from you, I was not the one who released her." He did not wish to cast a blight on Ruby's name, but Crispin would uncover the truth, he always did. Exhaustion pulled the truth from his lips as though it would purge the sin from his soul.

"If you were the only one privy to her location and her suspicious behavior, then pray tell, who released her if not you?" Crispin's patience grew thin. He leaned closer. "Tell me, Henry."

Bracing himself for his friend's anger, Henry closed his eyes. "Ruby discovered us in the north tower. She forged an agreement with Ivy. I know not what was said, but she released her and vowed she would take responsibility for the maid should it come to light."

When the strike did not come, Henry opened his eyes. Crispin rose to his feet and paced the small cell. His curses echoed off the stone. When he finally paused, he spun to face Henry.

"How could you allow her to be so reckless?" Crispin shouted, rage consuming him. "You should have brought Ivy to me." His fists clenched tight. If he held a sword, Henry would most surely have felt the blade.

After a time, Crispin's pacing slowed, his shouts became muttered curses, and Henry was finally able to relax without fear of Crispin turning on him in blind anger.

"I should have stopped her, my lord." Henry studied the dirt and blood caked upon his knuckles. "I was wrong to keep Ivy's treachery from you." He shook his head suppressing the tears once more. "Forgive me."

Crispin raked his hand through his hair and inhaled deeply. "What is done cannot be undone. But so help me, Henry, I cannot fathom why you would keep something such as this from me."

"I love her, sire." Henry's confession rang through the room.

"Of all the wenches in the kingdom, you give your heart to a spy and a traitor." Crispin scoffed. "Seems only fitting since your family betrayed the crown that you would choose a woman who would do the same."

Henry suppressed the heated rage filling him. "I knew nothing of my family's involvement in the raid meant to kill Ruby as a child. After everything we have encountered together, I remained by your side, steadfast and loyal to my own detriment." His hands balled into fists and his heart pounded hard against his ribs. "You think a pretty face is enough to tempt me to betray my king and country?"

Crispin regarded him thoughtfully. "I think you are human and as easily swayed as any other man when presented with a willing wench in his bed."

"Damn you," Henry spat, his hands trembling as the fury poured through him. "Have I not sacrificed enough to sate your demands for loyalty and honor?"

"You have sacrificed much, Henry. I do not question your loyalty, merely your reasoning and logic." Crispin grew solemn. "Did it not occur to you to be wary of anyone who sought your companionship? You are my right hand, my confidant, and my sole friend. If my enemies wished to get to me, they would surely use you. Did you not consider Ivy might be such a ruse to distract you from your duty? To gain entrance or allay your suspicions?"

Henry shut his eyes, wishing himself a thousand miles from this cell. "Every day I harbored these fears, bore them as a shield to protect myself. But Ivy...did not approach me. I seduced her.

How was I to know the truth?"

"When you found her in my presence chamber unattended." Crispin's accusation hung between them. "You should have brought her directly to me. I would have dealt with it accordingly."

His heart seized at the idea of Ivy facing punishment, even after her betrayals. He could not bring himself to cast her aside for the wolves to devour. "I should have, sire. I cannot undo the past, nor can I say with any certainty I would have done any differently should I have the opportunity to alter the past."

Crispin caught his head in his hands and groaned. "Tell me you had no knowledge of her agreement with Francis."

"When I questioned her, she refused to tell me whom she served and in what capacity. I could only assume she meant to bring harm to someone as her skills far surpass even the bravest knights in the kingdom." The tension in Henry's shoulders eased as the conversation shifted.

"If she was truly trained by the Guild, then I have no doubts she could have easily killed us whenever she chose." Crispin leaned back against the wall beside Henry. "Those trained by the Guild are rumored to be heartless assassins and masters of manipulation."

"Why did Francis not have her kill us and then reveal himself? It would have been much simpler than this game of power and persuasion he insists on playing." Henry tilted his head to study Crispin's profile.

"He is determined to have my reputation ruined completely." The realization came easily upon deeper reflection. Crispin plucked at his torn sleeve. "I was certainly on a path of self-destruction before my father banished me from the castle. His effort to save my soul, as it were, led me directly into Ruby's embrace. Had it not been for her, I would have found myself exactly where Francis intended. Ruined beyond any hope of salvation. The kingdom would have been forfeit, and he could have reappeared to take the throne without challenge."

Henry understood completely. Ruby had been an unanticipated factor in Francis's plans. Her joining Crispin hindered his long-awaited opportunity to return to the throne a hero as well as a savior. Francis's bold revelation nagged at his conscience.

"Tell me truly." Henry licked his lips, fearing the answer to the question burning in the back of his mind. "Did you hire someone to kill your father, Crispin?"

A shadow fell across Crispin's face. It could have merely been a trick of the light, but Henry noticed the shift in his friend's demeanor. For a moment, he feared he crossed a line and Crispin would lash out at him for even asking such a thing. Crispin finally hung his head.

"I paid a man in the village to find someone willing to take care of my father." His confession was soft but clear. Henry held his breath, unable and unwilling to break the spell cast around it. "I never intended to follow through with it. I was drunk and angry. I wanted to hurt him for punishing me. He wanted me to fill Francis's role." Crispin's voice rose with vehemence. "But I am not my sainted brother!"

Whatever hell Francis endured, he was no longer the same sainted, selfless man they once knew. He remembered their formative years training as knights fondly. Francis, Crispin, Henry, Simon, Timothy, Jacob, and several others who spent nearly all their time together both in the training ring and out.

Francis was the bastion of light. A golden knight dedicated to service and chivalry. Timothy and Jacob idolized him, following him like hounds come to heel. Simon was his closest friend and companion. So similar were they in stature and manner, people often confused them, a benefit Simon often used to his advantage when seducing sweet maidens at the local inn. While Crispin and Henry often followed in their wake, they remained together, set apart from the others, making their own way and often causing trouble in the process. No one could live up to the standard Francis set. No one ever tried. He was the golden prince.

"No one would blame you for wanting recognition on your own merits." Henry rested his hand on Crispin's shoulder in a show of solidarity. "If it helps, I do not think it was your fault the king died. There is no proof, nothing to tie you to his death. It does not help to dwell upon it."

Crispin faced Henry, his eyes rimmed with red and his cheek discolored from where the guards struck him. "When Francis tells my mother, it will not matter if I had a hand in it or not. She will never forgive me for even considering such a vile act." His breath hitched. "I cannot bear for her to look upon me with disgust and disappointment for such a betrayal."

Henry could find no words of comfort to soothe his friend's conscience. Instead, he relaxed beside him, and together they sat in silence. The echo of conversations filtered through the corridors, muffled by the stone and wood confining them. At least he was no longer alone. Now he had Crispin and they would find a solution. A way to free themselves and Ruby from Francis's vile plot.

"Do you remember?" Henry chuckled as a random memory assailed his weary mind. "When we were young and Francis was determined to ride your father's new destrier. Simon encouraged him to take the mammoth beast out into the field beyond the castle walls. Idiotic." His shoulders trembled with laughter making his sides ache.

Crispin snorted. "The horse threw him into a mud bog. It took all four of us to pull him out, and six hours to catch the temperamental beast. Father was livid."

"'Twas all Simon's idea too. He was such a horrible influence on Francis, on all of us." Henry's laughter subsided. "I shall never forget your mother's face when we returned covered from head to foot in mud, the stallion prancing behind us with pride."

"I thought she would thrash us all until we could not sit." Crispin chuckled. "We were what...all of eight years?"

"Francis, Simon, and Jacob were eleven. Timothy was the same age as us." Henry sighed, his soul lighter even though his body screamed, stiff and sore. "Such adventures we had."

"Aye." Crispin agreed, inhaling deeply. "But it does us no good to dwell on the past."

"I know." Henry shrugged. "But it does us good to laugh,

at least it distracts from the brutal reality of our situation for a moment."

"We must find a way to escape." Crispin turned serious. "We cannot accept this fate. He cannot win."

"We are his prisoners, Crispin." Henry gestured to the cell. "What would you have me do, conjure a miracle from the air?"

"Of course not, but I refuse to rot in this cell and concede defeat." He pushed himself off the bed and paced the cell as his mind began to churn with ideas. "We must escape and take Ruby with us."

Henry watched, exhausted but engaged. "We are but two men locked in a cell. I am useless in a fight as I am. Even if we escape, we have no allies, no army, no horses, and no weapons. We cannot return to the castle unprepared. He will surely be lying in wait for us."

Crispin leaned against the wall, his lips pursed. "Then we leave Meradin. We take Ruby and we leave. Seek asylum in England."

"You would abandon your throne, your kingdom...your people?" His jaw dropped at the declaration.

"Do you think I wish to abandon my people in their hour of need?" Crispin rounded on him. "We can save Ruby. We can escape. When the time is right, we can return and fight Francis, but I cannot do it if she is dead or worse...bound to him."

"If we attempt to escape, he will kill us." Henry despised the words as they left his tongue. Their fate hung in the balance, and nothing could stop the swing of the axe above their necks.

"We will be free or die trying to escape." Crispin straightened to his full height, his shoulders square and his chin held high. "I will die by my will, not by his."

Emboldened by his declaration, Henry nodded, and hope filled his chest. For the first time since Francis reappeared in their lives, they had direction and determination. "Tell me what to do."

Chapter Fourteen

For two days, Ruby remained trapped within a carriage, the windows and doors sealed from the outside. With only her thoughts for company, she replayed the events leading to this moment trying not to dwell on the impossibility of the insurmountable obstacles before her.

She leaned against the swaying carriage, taking comfort in the knowledge that they would soon reach their destination, and then she would be able to recruit aid to rescue Henry and Crispin.

There had been little time to react to the scene Ruby witnessed in Francis's makeshift throne room. Hearing the accusations hurled at Crispin stung even more than seeing him beaten and battered. The moment Francis had Crispin and Henry dragged from the room, she revolted turning on Francis with what little strength remained in her.

The guards put a stop to her assault quickly enough. One of them pinned her arms behind her back. She struggled against his hold, but it mattered not with his size and determination to protect Francis. Her screams and curses echoed through the room.

When Francis met her gaze, nothing of the once humble and timid monk remained in the depths of his vibrant, haunting eyes. Whoever that man had been was a lie. A well-crafted façade meant to create a sense of comfort and companionship. Ruby's stomach churned even now at the thought of the trust she placed in him over the years. Their comradery had been a deception. Although she would probably never know if he used her with purpose, or if their meeting had been a cruel twist of fate.

Francis spoke not to her, but to the guard who held her with simple instructions. Return her to her chamber and prepare the carriage.

Those words sent a shiver down her spine. What was he intending? Where was he going? Would he be taking her? What would happen to Crispin and Henry?

After being dragged to her chambers and locked inside, Ruby found a small trunk in the center of the room. Inside were garments he provided along with the clothes she wore the day they took her. Clean, of course, and neatly folded at the bottom of the trunk. Ruby searched the rest of the contents but could not find her dagger or her jeweled belt. Her heart sank at their absence.

The disappointment had not dissipated in two days. Neither had her fury at Francis for locking Crispin and Henry in the dungeon and then wrenching her from her chambers to be thrown in an airless carriage. Left with only her thoughts, Ruby replayed the conversation between Francis and Crispin over and over in her mind.

A thousand questions buffeted her, but all remained unanswered as time progressed. She could not be certain of how long they traveled, but the little bit of sustenance contained within the carriage dwindled to nearly nothing. The carriage reeked of sweat and piss. She tried to sleep, blocking out the scent, but the rough roads made rest an impossibility.

When the rocking ceased, Ruby straightened immediately, her body bracing for another onslaught of abuse. The carriage door opened, and sunlight streamed through, blinding her for a moment until her eyes adjusted to the brightness. A pair of hands reached into the tight compartment and pulled her out into the fresh air.

Ruby inhaled deeply, thankful for the rich scent of pine and dirt surrounding her. As her eyes adjusted, she recognized the forests around them. She shivered against the chill in the air even as the sunlight warmed her from above. Her stomach settled along with her mind, and for a brief moment, she felt free.

"Whatever thoughts are in your mind, I suggest you banish them." Francis's brusque command shattered the illusion.

Spinning around, Ruby searched for her captor. He stood beside a small cottage, wearing a simple tunic and hose with a plain doublet. Gone were the ostentatious garments he flaunted in hiding and the humble robes of the monk's order. The overgrown vines and thatched roof blended in with the surrounding brush, hiding the small building. He looked every thread a humble servant, not the villain she knew him to be. He leered, allowing his gaze to roam the length of her before speaking again.

"Inside you will find a bath, fresh garments, and some food." He unfolded his arms and stalked toward her.

Ruby stumbled back, colliding with one of her expressionless guards. "Where are you taking me?"

"Culver. Where we belong." His smile did not reach his eyes. "When we return to the castle, I shall tell the tale of how I rescued you from certain death. And you will remain silent if you wish to ensure the continued survival of both your loyal hounds."

A sliver of hope shone through the darkness. Crispin and Henry were alive, at least this is what Francis implied with his ominous threat. Before she could reach out and take hold of it, he crushed it beneath his boot.

"We have parts to play, Ruby. You and I." He leaned close. She cringed when his breath brushed over her skin. "Should you choose not to remain faithful to the story I choose to tell, I shall send word to have my men torture Henry first. They will strap him down and carve him like a wild boar, bit by bit while he screams for mercy." He licked his lips as though aroused by the mere thought of inflicting such agonizing pain.

A tear slipped from her eye. He continued, unrelenting in his passion.

"Then I shall set my men upon Crispin." Wicked intent glinted in his gleeful expression. "When they begin, I shall have them send the pieces wrapped in velvet. A reminder of your failure to save them."

How could this vile creature's twisted mind devise such a torment? More tears slipped free, but Ruby remained steadfast, refusing to show him how much his words affected her.

"Do you understand the consequences of your actions

should you fail to adhere to the details I provide?" Francis cocked his head, waiting.

"I do." The response was soft and trembled with emotion, but Ruby could not form any other words. There was no pleading. No begging. She could not argue with a monster. If she wished to fight against him, it would take an act of God and a band of heavenly hosts to send this tormented soul to hell where he belonged. Defeated, Ruby hung her head.

"Very good." He stepped aside and gestured toward the cottage. "You must prepare for our arrival."

Desperate to be away from him, Ruby entered the cottage. Emma and Eva glanced up from their tasks as she closed the door behind her.

"Come, pet." Emma rushed forward to help her disrobe.

A steaming bath lay before the small hearth. Ruby conceded to their instruction, allowing them to lead her to the bath, wash and dress her, and then feed her as though she were an invalid child.

Her mind replayed Francis's threat over and over searching for any possibility of deception. But it was hopeless. He intended to follow through with every horrific threat.

Once they left the cottage, Ruby was relieved to see the carriage had vanished. In its place were two horses. Francis was already astride the dark chestnut gelding. He motioned to the gray dappled gelding Ruby recognized as Ghost. Why would he take Ghost of all horses? The servants would surely recognize Crispin's horse. She pushed aside the thought and, with one of the guard's help, settled in the saddle.

Ghost danced beneath her. Being in the saddle once more revitalized her. She missed this. It would only take a nudge to send Ghost into a gallop and race ahead to the castle.

"Remember my promise, Ruby." Francis's voice cut through the haze of her half-hatched plan.

Instead of testing his resolve, Ruby nodded, choosing instead to wait for an opportunity that would not only ensure her success but reveal his duplicitous nature to the whole kingdom.

Francis led the way, and Ruby followed behind. Her gaze

fixed on the road and not on the man before her. She would find a way. There was no other alternative. Crispin and Henry would not come to her rescue. She would have to come to theirs.

Even if she were able to convince Vivienne to send knights, she had no idea of the location where Francis had held her and now kept his prisoners. God's blood, he was clever. Keeping her in a concealed carriage for part of the journey and then allowing her to arrive as though she were rescued.

Ruby indulged in a vivid fantasy of herself burying a blade in the bastard's back. She only hoped when the time came, she could be the one to end him. Justice for what he had done to her and her unborn child.

She refused to allow the grief to take control once more. There would be time to grieve afterward. Ruby focused instead on the situation at hand. She needed a plan. What would the Lady of the Forest do? How would she deal with such a villain?

The sun set, and they still had not reached Culver. Ruby shifted in the saddle, trying to glimpse the castle through the bare trees. The sliver of the moon hid behind the clouds overhead. A lantern swung from a pole attached to Francis's saddle, casting light across the road ahead.

Relief filled her when they reached the village. The streets lay deserted as they wove through.

As they approached the main portcullis, a sentry of guards stood before them. One of the men addressed Francis.

"State your business." His drawn sword glinted in the torchlight.

"I have returned with the queen and news of the king." Francis's reply shattered the silence.

The guards burst into agitated murmurs and moved aside. After a few frantic shouts, they motioned for the gate to open and waved Francis onward.

Ruby's face heated at their curious gazes. She passed by forcing herself to wear a gracious smile and not scream for help. Once they reached the inner bailey, news of their return had spread through the castle.

Servants spilled from every corner of the bailey. When Ruby

glimpsed the familiar faces, her heart nearly shattered with overwhelming relief. She feared she would never see them again. Matthew appeared by her side, taking the reins from her hands.

"Praise be the Saints," he murmured as he helped her down from the saddle. "We thought you were dead, my lady."

Ruby's hands trembled under his kind touch. The ground nearly gave out beneath her. Matthew caught her before she fell.

"Let me help you." He passed off the reins to a page and offered his support.

Ruby leaned into his strength, drawing from it allowing it to fortify her. This was the first true selfless act of kindness she had experienced since this ordeal began.

"Thank you, Matthew." She straightened but clung to him unable to bear the thought of facing Francis again.

"What goes on here?" Vivienne's question cut through the curious chatter of the crowd gathered in the bailey. She drew to a stop when her gaze fell on Francis. "What...?" Then she saw Ruby. She rushed forward and wrapped Ruby in a warm, comforting embrace. "Oh, my dear." She gasped through her choked sob.

Ruby could say nothing. She clung to Vivienne and allowed the tears to fall unchecked. Relief and a mixture of conflicting emotions congealed in her chest. All she could do was bask in the soothing embrace of someone who truly loved her.

Vivienne stroked her hair. "We were so worried about you." She drew back to search Ruby's face. Her fingertips caressed her cheek and tears filled her eyes. "Praise be, you have returned." After a long moment, she disentangled herself and glanced at Francis.

Ruby cringed at the look of confusion on her lovely face.

"Where is Crispin? And Henry?" Vivienne put a voice to the question burning in the minds of every soul in the bailey.

"Mother." Francis stepped forward, his humble façade firmly in place. "Crispin has betrayed us all."

Ruby's stomach revolted at the knowledge of his duplicity and yet remained silent. Her hands clenched into fists beneath her cloak. No matter how much she longed to unveil his lies, she would not endanger the lives of the men who remained under his control.

"'Tis not possible." Vivienne covered her mouth stunned into silence, her eyes wide.

"I loathe bringing you such distressing news." Francis bowed low in a show of humility. "I saw him turn with my own eyes. Heard the truth from his lips. The king has forsaken his country and his queen."

His proclamation had a profound effect on the crowd. A ripple of whispers cascaded over those standing in the bailey. As much as she loathed his deceit, she recognized the mastery of his plan. Revealing Crispin's betrayal in such a manner planted the seed of doubt while also bolstering Francis's claim to the throne and solidifying his role as her savior. By the morrow, the whole of Culver would hear the tale, and by week's end, the kingdom of Meradin.

Ruby dug her nails into her palms to keep from defending Crispin's honor and exposing Francis's plot.

"Come inside," Vivienne directed, giving both her and Francis her familiar matronly grimace of distaste. She knew the consequences of such a revelation in the midst of the crowd and sought to mitigate it. The Queen Mother was no fool. Ruby could only hope Francis underestimated his mother as much as he did her.

With a longing glance over her shoulder at Matthew who stood stroking Ghost's neck, Ruby followed Vivienne's lead, seeking comfort as she took Ruby by the arm and escorted her inside the great hall. Francis stepped into her view, his gaze stern and filled with warning.

Vivienne took charge shouting directions to the stunned servants. A flurry of activity surrounded them as they worked quickly to secure several seats before the oversized hearth and retrieved food from the kitchen.

Ruby sat beside Vivienne, putting as much distance between herself and Francis as she could. To all the rest of those present, he was the epitome of graciousness and humility. But she marked the sly glances he bestowed upon her ensuring she

"The servants will tend to your comfort. Francis, I must see Ruby is safely settled."

"I will pray for your recovery, my lady." Francis's mask slipped for a brief moment, and she gasped at the look of warning he flashed before slipping his façade back into place.

Once she and Vivienne reached her chamber, Ruby collapsed onto the bed and allowed the tears to come. Vivienne settled down beside her and drew her into her arms.

"You are safe, darling. Shhh. Hush now. Just rest." Her gentle touch and soothing words calmed Ruby. Her sobs stilled into delicate hiccoughs. Exhaustion pulled her deeper into its weighted embrace.

Vivienne tucked her into bed and called for her young maid to bring fresh water and food after stoking the fire. She retreated from the room, leaving Ruby alone with Mina.

"Mina," Ruby called the sweet, young girl to her side.

"My lady. We were so worried about you." Mina took her hand. Her tender smile warmed Ruby's heart.

"I need you to do something for me." She squeezed the girl's hand. "Take a message to Matthew, the smith's apprentice."

"What shall I tell him, my lady?" Her eyes widened.

"Marian must gather the rosemary for Guy." Ruby blinked away the returning tears.

"I do not understand," Mina pleaded. "What does it mean?"

"He will know what to do. Now go. Quickly. Return once you have delivered the message." She prayed it would succeed. "I wish for you to remain by my side."

"As you wish, my lady." Mina darted out the door, closing it firmly behind her.

Ruby collapsed on the bed. The serpent was beneath their roof. She could not reveal him directly, but with such intricate lies, he undoubtedly would reveal himself. When he did, she would be prepared.

Chapter Fifteen

The walls trembled from the force of Crispin's shouts. Woken from the depths of a restless sleep, Henry searched the dark cell. His good eye adapted quickly while the other refused to even open. His body ached, and the gnawing hunger in his gut refused to relent. The thought of a drop of cool spring water made him moan.

Crispin spun around from his position beside the door. "Remain there. Moan louder and clutch your head."

Confusion clouded Henry's understanding. "What?"

"I have a plan." Crispin tried to pry at the slot in the door where the guards would typically deliver food or water to prisoners. Only they had not delivered a scrap since they locked them inside. Had they been left for dead?

"What plan?" Henry groaned as he shifted his head.

"The escape plan." Crispin pressed his fingers to his lips. "Trust me."

Henry was in no position to argue. They had no other alternative. After searching the cell numerous times, from the ceiling to the floor, they found no loose stone or bricks to use as weapons and no secrets hidden within the walls. Their only hope of escape lay through the solid door bolted from the outside.

Crispin shouted again, the sound ringing through Henry's head. He moaned loudly, but the pain was sincere. The narrow cell did nothing to dull the amplification of their voices. When Crispin raised his voice, Henry wished the sainted archangels would claim him. Anything to stop the torment.

"*Help!*" Crispin's pleas reverberated off the walls. He pounded his fists upon the door. "Come quickly!" The touch of panic in his voice told Henry the cries were not completely fabricated.

Henry knew this game well. The plea for assistance for a

wounded companion would garner sympathy, assuming their guards even had a conscience or a soul. If they would die here, would that not ruin Francis's plans? He stifled a chuckle at the fleeting thought even as it grew into a burgeoning reality.

He threw himself into the role. Moaning and thrashing upon the rickety bed. Henry half feared it would break and the pieces of wood might impale him. At least it would end his suffering. Or prolong it? He shivered at the possibility before shoving it away.

"Do you even have a weapon should someone respond?" Henry asked between grunting cries of agony made purely for emphasis on his perceived condition.

Crispin pointedly ignored him, instead focusing on redoubling his efforts to break down the door with his bare fists. His voice grew hoarse with the continued shouts for help.

Henry felt what little strength he possessed slip away. If he lost consciousness again, then what use would he be? He forced himself to remain alert. They must...escape...He took a deep breath and his eyes drifted closed, pulling him into the blissful abyss.

The slide and thud of the wooden slat opening jerked him back from the edge of surrender. A solitary beam of light shone through the slat until a shadow fell over it.

"What goes on here?" a woman's voice snapped.

Ivy. Henry's heart twisted at the sound of her voice. He tried to sit up, but the motion only threw his body into torment. He writhed on the bed and groaned in agony.

The shadow disappeared. "Open this door. Now!" Her command echoed through the tiny window. A jangle of keys and the slide of wood and metal was the reply to her order.

Crispin stepped aside, unable to hide or sidestep away as the door swung open. Her silhouette filled the door frame.

Henry never saw anything as beautiful or as terrifying as her dressed in hose and a tunic brandishing her dagger. A halo of light surrounded her like an avenging angel come to Earth. She stepped into the room, her blade ready and her gaze focused on Crispin alone.

"Back against the wall." She stepped into the cell. Two guards filled the gaping doorway their hands on their hilts, waiting for her instructions. Ivy gestured toward the wall. "Now."

With measured steps, Crispin did as she commanded. His one hand braced against the wall and the other raised high.

Ivy's gaze remained fixed on Crispin. "'Tis wise to know when you have been beaten, *Your Majesty*." Her sneering emphasis on his formal address showed her disdain for the man before her.

How could he have loved someone with such hatred in their soul? Even worse, how had he not seen beyond the obvious lies? Shame washed over him. He pinched his eyes closed. Another burst of tension pulled at his skull. He gripped his head, wishing he could remove it and ease the pressure. When he opened his eyes, they encountered her luminous green gaze.

For the briefest moment, he glimpsed the heart beneath the layers of steel. The heart he once held in his hands. Or so he thought.

"Ivy." Her name caressed his lips as a prayer whispered to the heavens. If this were the end, it would only be fitting she be the one to do so. One merciful stroke would end his suffering. No strength to plead or beg remained. Surrender came easily knowing she held the blade.

"Henry...I..." The flash of sympathy in her eyes dissipated like rose petals amid a raging storm.

A blur of movement forced Henry to right himself. Crispin lunged forward, catching Ivy by the arm. The struggle for the dagger lasted a breath. Henry gasped at the small blade pressed against Ivy's throat. Her weapon clattered to the floor. Moving quickly, Henry bent to retrieve it before the two guards burst into the room.

"Drop your weapons." Crispin's demand cut through the scuffle. "Drop them or I slit her throat."

"Kill her." The first guard snapped. That voice. Henry strained to get a better look at the guards.

He gasped. "Donnal? Richard? It cannot be." Henry

staggered to his feet, bracing his hand against the wall until the ground ceased swaying beneath him.

His eldest brother sneered. "We should kill them now. Save us the trouble."

"Those were not our instructions," Ivy barked, struggling against Crispin's hold. His grip on her tightened. A trickle of blood slid down her throat. She stilled, but her focus remained on his brothers.

He should have known after the ceremony when they disappeared. They would ally with the one person who could absolve them.

"Traitorous bastards," Henry spat. "I hope you burn in hell."

"I will not tell you again," Crispin interjected, steering the conversation back. "Drop. Your. Weapons. Do not test my resolve."

"Do as he says, damn you! 'Twill be your hide if he kills me." Ivy speared them with an icy glare. "My master has not released me from his service. He will be most displeased if he finds his most prized possession slaughtered at the hands of your prisoner."

Henry's brothers hesitated for a moment before tossing aside their weapons. The satisfaction of hearing the steel clatter on the stone bolstered Henry's courage.

"Can you make it?" Crispin whispered.

Henry met Crispin's gaze and nodded. Ivy remained still, her attention riveted on Henry's brothers in the doorway. Mustering whatever reserves he possessed, Henry rose to his full height and gripped the dagger in his fist.

"Out of the way." Henry led the way, shoving aside his brothers. He searched them for any remaining weapons and then pushed them into the cell. A thrill of satisfaction burned through him when he slid the bolt home and removed the key from the padlock.

The two men beat on the door, their shouts muffled by the thick wood. Henry hazarded a smile, but it faded as quickly as it appeared. 'Twas too simple. Far too simple. He slid the slat closed with a thud and turned to face Crispin.

"What?" His friend searched his face, his grip still firm on their prisoner.

"That was far too simple." Henry shifted his attention to Ivy. "How many remain?" When she refused to respond, he grasped her chin in his hand, bringing her close. "Tell me or I will kill you myself."

The face he once loved revealed not a flicker of emotion. A piece of his soul died at the realization she did not care for him and never did. He shook her but she refused to reply.

"Where is the queen?" Crispin tightened his grip, making Ivy gasp at the pressure of the blade against her throat.

"Gone."

"Where?"

"Culver."

"Gather the weapons," Crispin interjected. "We shall rid ourselves of this burden and make our own escape."

Guilt and panic clawed at his throat. For all his threats, Henry could not bring himself to actually murder the woman he loved. Instead, he stalked to the neighboring cell and swung the door open.

Without prompting, Crispin tossed her inside and shut the door. Henry slid the bolt home and locked the door.

"Come." Henry handed a sword to Crispin.

"Are you able to ride?" Crispin's concern warmed Henry to his core.

He gave a firm nod.

"Then let us away." Crispin clapped his hand on Henry's shoulder. He turned and crept up the stairs.

Henry followed closely. The receding sounds of his brothers' shouting faded into a distant memory. Once they reached the main corridor, Crispin clung to the wall, his mission clear. Escape.

The castle lay deserted around them. Once they reached the inner bailey, Crispin stopped short. A faint sound of conversation drifted through the cracked door.

"How many?" Henry whispered.

"Five, perhaps six." Crispin motioned toward the opposite wall. "If we exit through the kitchen, we may find a way to escape through the rear."

Henry and Crispin remained in the shadows as they wove through the labyrinth of the unfamiliar castle. The kitchen lay deserted. Francis did not have much support in his quest to seize the throne. At least at this point. Once he infested the kingdom with his lies, the people would turn on Crispin. They must reach the castle and unmask him before it was too late.

Outside, the sun dipped below the tree line. If they made it into the forest, they could remain hidden with ease. Horses would have been useful, but they could not take the chance of stealing horses from the stables and drawing attention to themselves.

"This way." Crispin followed the outer wall, taking shelter behind barrels and crates stacked along the path.

Ducking behind a large crate, they waited until the guard at the postern gate stopped to piss along the far side of the wall. The rushing sound of water over rocks filtered through the air. Quietly, they slipped through the doorway and out onto a rocky ledge, below lay a river.

A narrow path led around the side of the castle wide enough for a single horse cart. If they followed it to the woods, they could easily be caught if their escape from the dungeon were noticed.

"Which way?" Henry leaned against the stone wall.

"Who goes there?" A guard appeared over the side of the wall. He disappeared when he could not locate the source of the noise. They were caught.

Henry's heart raced. He would rather die than subject himself to the confines of the cell at the hands of his family and Francis. "Jump."

Crispin's jaw set as though reaching the same conclusion.

Without another moment's hesitation, Henry jumped into the frigid waters of the rushing river. The icy water bit into his flesh, soothing and scalding simultaneously. He struggled to right himself, but the current swept him away.

He battled to keep his head above the water. Arms flailing and chest convulsing, he fought. The castle faded into a small pinprick in the distance as the river carried him downstream. His body sank into a numb void, and he slipped beneath the surface surrendering to his fate.

Chapter Sixteen

The river surged around him, pushing and pulling like a flag whipping in the wind. His clothes absorbed the cold water and weighed him down. Distant shouts echoed behind him, lost in the sounds of the water crashing against the rocks. Crispin searched for Henry, who had jumped in first.

Henry vanished beneath the surface. He had been so weak already, too much time spent in this frigid water would certainly kill him. Panic clutched at his chest, sinking into his bones like the icy embrace of the river. He dove beneath the surface grasping for whatever he found.

Hindered by the sword in his hand, Crispin fought the current and the cold. When something soft collided with his thigh, he dove beneath the water and grasped it. Breaking the surface, Crispin gasped for air and groaned using all his strength to pull.

Henry's limp body broke the surface. Crispin held tight and swam toward shore. When his feet found the river bottom, he pushed harder. With his sights set on a small outcropping of trees, Crispin pulled Henry from the water.

The cold air against his wet skin made his teeth chatter. He pushed aside the discomfort and deposited Henry in the grass beside the river. Crispin collapsed beside him. He shook Henry, discouraged by the tint of blue beneath his skin. He felt for any signs of life, but nothing.

"Breathe, damn you." Crispin beat his fist on Henry's chest. Water dripped from his hair, spattering on his friend's pale, lifeless face. "I forbid you abandon me now." The panic turned to anguish in his gut and a sob wrenched from his throat. Tears mingled with the water trailing over his cheek.

In defiance, Crispin grasped Henry by the shirt and hoisted him across his lap. "You cannot die. Not now. Not when you are the only person I can trust." He shook him again. "Henry." Resignation filled his voice. His friend was gone.

Fury engulfed him. Rage replaced the grief hovering in the back of his mind. He touched his friend's cheek gently before rolling him aside and climbing to his feet. He could not remain here. They would soon come searching for him.

Movement by his feet made him jump. Henry twitched retching water into the grass. He gasped and color filled his cheeks.

"You glorious bastard." Crispin dropped to his friend's side and helped him rise. "I thought you died and left me to do all the damned work."

Henry's teeth chattered and his lips were still a soft shade of blue, but he smiled. After another bought of coughing and retching water, he glanced at Crispin.

Relief filled him. Henry was not dead. He would live, but they needed to find shelter. A place to hide and warm themselves until dark. Then they could return to the castle. Crispin had little idea where they were and how long their journey would take.

"Can you walk?" Crispin tugged on his friend's shirt. "We need to seek shelter. Get out of these wet clothes and find something to eat."

Henry nodded, struggling to climb to his feet. Crispin grasped his friend by the arm and came around him offering support. He grabbed the discarded sword, and together they pushed through the brush into the forest.

The deeper they ventured into the thicket, the sound of the river slowly faded. Henry trembled with each step, his skin cold and damp.

"O—ver the—re." Henry stuttered and struggled to get the words out. But Crispin recognized a small structure through the trees ahead.

Together they limped toward it, praying it was abandoned.

As they approached, the building came into view. A barn tucked into a small clearing. Beyond it, a cottage stood with smoke billowing up from the chimney. Not abandoned, but they would have to take their chances. Henry's steps grew heavier with each passing moment spent in the cold.

When they reached the cottage, Crispin pounded on the door. "Is anyone here?"

It opened beneath his hand. A dour, but familiar face appeared. The northern villager from the night of the feast. The man's scowl disappeared instantly. "Your majesty, what are—?" His gaze took in Crispin's soaking form and then fell on Henry. "Come in."

Crispin carried Henry into the cottage and deposited him in front of the fire. "My thanks. I do not wish to impose, but he will not survive unless—" The words choked him. He refused to think on it.

"I shall gather some blankets." The man jumped into action, leaving Crispin to peel the nearly frozen clothes from his friend's trembling form.

Henry closed his eyes and let Crispin work. The warmth from the fire brought comfort. He prayed it did the same for Henry, who was far too weak from the ordeal to speak. The older man returned as Crispin peeled the remaining fabric from over Henry's head. He wrapped a warm blanket around him and set to removing his own wet clothes.

"What happened, sire?" The man placed a soft cushion beneath Henry's head where he lay before the fire.

"The queen was taken. We tracked them to a keep up the river but were captured as well." Crispin modified the tale enough to sate the man's curiosity but kept the details vague. "We managed to escape and ended up in the river." He shrugged and hung his wet clothes near the fire.

"And the queen?" The man's soft voice solidified Crispin's resolve. "Where is she?"

"Gone," Crispin growled. "Taken again." He pushed aside his failure and focused instead on the task at hand. With the blanket wrapped around him, the heat finally began absorbing into his flesh.

"How may I be of service, your majesty?" He looked much like he did the night he arrived at the doorstep of the castle the night of the feast requesting aid.

"Where are the soldiers I sent?" Crispin asked, distracted by the juncture in which they found themselves.

"In the village. They have secured it for the moment, but I fear the bandits will return once more when they depart." The man shook his head and retrieved two bowls from a shelf beside the fire.

"I see." Crispin pondered his words. Until he purged Francis, he could do nothing to ensure the safety of his people. Francis enlisted the Balmonts' aid, promising them absolution from their prior sins. There would be reckoning for their betrayal.

"I have some venison stew and some bread. It may not be much, but it will warm you and give you strength." The villager ladled stew from the steaming pot hanging next to the fire. He handed the bowl to Crispin.

"'Tis much appreciated." The scent and heat infused him instantly. "My thanks."

The man stared at him for a long moment before nodding. He crouched beside Henry and nudged him. Henry's eyes fluttered open focusing on Crispin and then their host.

"Eat." He held the bowl to Henry's lips.

They ate together in silence. Henry fell asleep almost instantly after he finished his stew. Crispin sat staring into the flames. They needed to get into the castle unnoticed. Once he breached the walls, he could turn his men on Francis.

There was only one way into the castle without being seen, and Francis knew of it. If he were wise, he would seal it the moment he returned to the castle. Crispin prayed his brother forgot the secret they kept since childhood. As the plan blossomed in his mind, he made a list of the items he would require and presented them to their gracious, if unwilling, host.

"Oh, and I will need to borrow two horses," Crispin added. "I shall have them returned post-haste once I reach Culver."

"Take whatever you need, sire." The man bowed. "I am your humble servant."

Once darkness fell, they had gathered the necessary supplies and saddled the horses. Crispin donned his dry clothes and woke

Henry.

"We must leave. Can you ride?" Crispin searched his friend's weary face. "Ruby is depending on us."

Henry gave a curt nod and slowly rose to his feet. He wobbled at the motion but held out his hand to stop Crispin from coming to his aid. "I can dress myself."

"Very well." Crispin took the borrowed cloak and stepped outside to find the man standing with the horses. "Your kindness has been dually noted."

"My thoughts and prayers are with the queen. I hope you locate her swiftly." He handed the reins to Crispin. "May God grant you mercy on your quest."

Henry stumbled from the cottage and mounted the other horse.

Crispin tipped his head in salute before urging the horse into a trot toward the path leading into the forest. If they rode hard enough, they could make it to Culver before nightfall on the morrow. He glanced at his companion who swayed in the saddle but held tight to the reins.

The thin smile on Henry's lips told Crispin what he needed to know. His friend was weak and exhausted, but he would see this through. They had already come so far. A bit farther, and they could finally end this.

When they reached the king's road, Crispin and Henry pushed their mounts hard. There would be no stopping until they reached Culver.

After hours in the saddle, they reached Tinley village before sundown the following evening. Half a league along the king's road would bring them to Culver. Crispin routed his horse on a disused path around the village.

Even though he believed them to be safely locked in his dungeon, Francis would have his men positioned around the area to keep watch. At least that was how they had been taught to think defensively, if Francis remembered anything of their training, of course. Crispin refused to take any chances.

He glanced over his shoulder to ensure Henry followed. His companion slumped forward on his horse. The trials of his ordeal took their toll. Crispin prayed he had enough strength to reach the keep. They had come so far already.

His friend's fortitude stunned him. After days of torture, beaten and starved, Henry remained steadfast. Even challenging death after nearly drowning in the river was not enough to tempt the man to betray his post. 'Twould have been easier for him to surrender to that fate, and yet he persevered. Such determination to survive was admirable, but Crispin knew every man had limits. He could not continue at this pace without suffering irreparable damage to his health...or submitting to death.

Once he caught sight of the familiar parapets and stone walls, Crispin breathed with relief. He brought his horse to a small clearing and allowed him to graze. Henry attempted to follow suit but collapsed as he dismounted.

"Just a bit further." Crispin wrapped his arm around his friend, hoisting him up. They quietly made their way through the thick trees to a spot on the far hilltop giving them a level view of the castle.

Torches stood bright along the walls, providing the only illumination for him to take measure of the fortifications. The clouds banished the moonlight which gave them a distinct disadvantage, but it could also be to their benefit when they attempted to breach the walls.

Henry lay on his back beside Crispin, his eyes closed, his breaths shallow. How could he ask his friend to push through his obvious pain to mount a rescue? He allowed him to rest as he scoured the castle's outer walls.

He frowned. Crispin saw no difference between the number of guards he utilized and what protected the keep now. Would Francis be so confident in his plan as to leave himself vulnerable? Perhaps, but if the past were any indication, Crispin knew there were unseen elements at work. He underestimated his brother before. There would not be another occasion.

A soft snore belied Henry's state of preparation. Crispin shook his head and allowed his friend to rest. Since the sun had just set, 'twas too soon to attempt to infiltrate the castle. They would wait several hours when he could be certain of the residents' slumber before attempting to gain entry.

Tempted to rest himself, Crispin could not ease his mind. His precious Ruby lay beyond those walls. He longed to see her again, hold her in his arms. Seeing her broken had nearly shattered his heart. Even though she possessed inner strength, her experience would most certainly take a toll upon her both physically and mentally. Should Francis intend to take her for his own, he would be in for a dangerous challenge. His Ruby would not go quietly. No amount of torture or threats would weaken her resolve. Of this he was certain given her past.

Crispin left Henry to sleep and ventured back to where the horses grazed. Halfway down the hill, a distinct prickle of unease stabbed at his conscience. He searched the trees around him, finding dark shadows and tall spires reaching into the heavens. The unease continued.

Someone watched him. He drew the dagger from his belt and held it tight in his fist. Moving forward, he watched for any indication of life in the darkness. A flicker of movement behind a wide trunk caught his eye. He crept forward and grasped at the flutter of fabric behind the tree.

The fabric broke loose in his hand. Crispin froze at the press of steel against his ribs. He lifted his hands and cursed beneath his breath.

"I entrusted her to your care." The blade dug deeper, making Crispin hiss. "And you failed."

Crispin turned slowly to face Marian. "I did, and for that, I beg your forgiveness."

Even in the darkness, he did not miss the flicker of surprise in her expression. She lowered her blade and he breathed in relief. If anyone would run him through without hesitation, it would be Marian. Ruby's mother was a force to be feared with reverence and respect. She wore all black, from the tunic down to her boots and a warm woolen cloak. As matronly as she seemed, he saw the same fire in her eyes he glimpsed in Ruby's.

"Until this is resolved, I cannot give you the absolution you seek." Marian sheathed her blade and grabbed his doublet in her fist. Her gaze searched his face for a long moment before she released him. "You look like you have faced the devil himself and lived to tell the tale."

Her assessment of his state was not incorrect, but he did not wish to dwell upon it. "What are you doing in the forest? Why are you not inside the castle with Ruby?"

"Yester eve Matthew appeared at my cottage bearing a message from Ruby." Marian retreated into the forest.

Crispin followed. "What was the message?"

"She requested I gather the rosemary for Guy." Her simple response struck him as odd.

"What the devil does that mean?" Crispin scowled and lumbered along behind her.

Marian sighed as they approached the horses. "Long ago, I fell in love with a dangerous man. We were caught between loyalties. My allegiance did not align with his. But I loved him, more than any reason could define." She sighed and turned to face him. A dim ethereal glow radiated around her, and Crispin saw the faded beauty of the woman she used to be.

"What does this have to do with the message?"

"Guy was hated by nearly every person in the land. When he turned on the sheriff, he was imprisoned and sentenced to hang." She cocked her head and sadness filled her eyes. "I abandoned everything I had ever known to rescue him from certain death. We escaped to Meradin and started a new life together."

Confused, Crispin ran his hand over his jaw. "I do not understand what this has to do with Ruby or the situation at present."

Marian pulled a sprig of rosemary from her pocket and held it up between them. "Rosemary is for remembrance. 'Tis a powerful herb, one my husband favored as well as Ruby."

"How does this help us?" He conceded ignorance, unable to grasp the meaning of her tale.

"The message was a warning for me to stay away. She did not want me to risk myself in coming to her aid." Marian smiled, but it was tainted by sadness and longing. When she met his gaze, defiance burned in the depths of her knowing eyes. "I would willingly trade my life for hers. She is the Lady of the Forest, the rightful queen of Meradin, the Protector of the People."

Understanding cascaded through him like the warmth of the summer sun, and he nodded. "As would I."

"I know, my son." She rested her hand on his shoulder. "Now, tell me what has transpired."

As they gathered supplies from the horses, Crispin explained the events since the night of the feast. Marian listened in silence. He attempted to keep the details simple and direct, but the more he spoke, the deeper it carved the effects into his memory. He abhorred how it made him seem weak and ineffective, but this was no confession for his soul, merely a revelation of the truth. A truth he had been unwilling to face for years.

Crispin, as selfish and vain as he seemed, was not an island unto himself. Henry and Ruby were his pillars of strength. Once he would have shunned the idea of being tied so deeply to another person, of being responsible for them. Being on the verge of losing them nearly brought him to his knees. They revealed a side of him he had never been willing to accept.

Silence descended between them when Crispin finished his tale. Marian walked beside him as they returned to the spot where he had left Henry.

"May God have mercy on us all," she murmured as they crested the ridge, bringing the castle into view. "This will be no simple task, Crispin. You will need to bring the past to light, free yourself from the lies binding you. Only then can you stake your claim with a clear conscience."

"Francis's lies will infect the privy council. They will turn against me." Crispin raked his hand through his hair. "Perhaps I should do as you did. Take Ruby and leave Meradin."

"Is that truly what you wish? To relinquish your throne, surrender to the man who used subversion and deceit to steal everything you hold dear." Marian gripped his arm. "He ripped your child from her womb without remorse and gloated."

The reminder lit a fire in his belly. A low rumbling growl reverberated in his throat at the thought of making Francis suffer for his insidious actions. His child and heir, stolen from him. His wife, broken and grief-stricken. The memory of Ruby's beautiful tear-stained face remained seared in his mind. She suffered deeply because of Francis. As did Henry. They deserved vengeance for the horrors they endured.

"What I wish is for my brother to suffer as punishment for what he has done." His fists clenched by his sides. His gaze fell on Henry as they approached. "They deserve peace."

Marian followed his gaze and nodded. "Aye." She knelt in the grass beside Henry and gently woke him with a nudge.

"Who—?" His groggy expression faded when he saw Marian. He relaxed against the grass. "Am I dead?"

"Most assuredly not dead." Marian reached into the bag on her hip and removed a small flagon. "Drink this. 'Twill restore your strength."

Henry sat up and took a deep drink. He grimaced at the taste but consumed it without question. "My thanks."

"Both of you will need some rest if we are to venture into the lion's den." She gestured to the grass. "Sleep. I shall keep watch."

"Do we have a plan?" Henry glanced at Crispin. "We cannot just walk up to the gate and demand entry. Francis will have planted his lies already and put the guards on watch for any that may be loyal to Crispin."

"He has done as much already." Marian sighed. "You both have been branded traitors to the crown. My little mouse inside the castle informed me earlier."

Crispin smiled. Of course, she would have eyes and ears inside the castle. Marian was truly a resourceful woman. His admiration for her grew with every revelation.

Henry threw his hands up. "Then how the devil do we gain entry if no one will listen to reason?"

"Oh, they will listen." Crispin stroked his hand along his jaw. "Once we locate Ruby, we will make them see reason."

"And how do you intend to breach the walls?" Henry pressed his lips together.

"Trust me." He gave his friend a firm pat on the shoulder.

"We will have Ruby and be gone before anyone realizes it."

Henry collapsed against the grass. "Trust is not the issue. But you are daft if you think we can find a way past the guards. I trained them myself. There is no way anyone is getting through."

Crispin and Marian exchanged a long look before she nodded.

"Sleep. I shall wake you in a few hours." Marian took watch beside them.

As he settled into the grass beside Henry, Crispin fought against the apprehension building in his chest. 'Twould be simple to snatch Ruby from Francis's hold and escape without notice. But deep in the pit of his stomach, he knew his conscience would never allow him to find peace if he did not interject on behalf of the people of Meradin.

Ruby was not the only one in danger. They all were. Francis would not be complacent with being king, he would be a tyrant. And Crispin could not allow his kingdom to fall to ruin at the hands of such a villain. But if he killed his brother, he would create a martyr and become the criminal everyone believed him to be.

Perhaps it would be wiser to run and leave Meradin forever, but could he subject Ruby to a life in exile as a wanted criminal? Either way, a battle lay on the horizon, and for once his fears lay not for himself but those he loved.

Chapter Seventeen

"The bruises are fading, my queen." Mina's innocent comment left Ruby unsteady.

She nodded as the young maid aided her in donning the heavy blue velvet gown trimmed with ermine fur. 'Twould keep her warm, but she loathed anything Francis chose for her.

Having returned to the castle, she allowed her mind to tuck aside the horrible events of the past fortnight. It would not do to dwell on them while Francis still held sway over the kingdom. Over the past several nights, she watched him methodically taint every aspect of life inside the keep.

His instructions for her clothing and her daily routine burrowed beneath her skin, but 'twas his demand she surrender all her weapons which left her bitter. He insisted with grand statements it would ensure her safety. She attempted to hide a dagger in her chamber, but he searched it thoroughly and found the blade stashed beneath the frame of her bed.

The unspoken threat hung heavy in the air. He would kill Crispin and Henry if she should cross him. Even mentioning them or the details of her ordeal would earn her a harsh punishment. He also restricted her time with Vivienne. Of course, he spun a tale of how she required rest to recover after such a harrowing experience.

In the few moments she spent with Vivienne, Ruby saw the tension bracketing her mouth, knowing she held her tongue. How could she speak out against one of her sons when the other was branded a traitor? Ruby longed to comfort her with the truth, but it would shatter the illusion of her elder son. There would be no easy way to address such a conundrum.

If only she had her mother to give her guidance, something to ease the painful twisting unease in her chest. She smoothed her hand over the soft skirts as Mina laced the gown.

"Have you spoken to Matthew since yestereve?" Ruby asked, her voice low. Francis posted guards outside her room, and she took every precaution to ensure they were unable to overhear her conversation with her maid.

"Aye, your highness. I passed him this morning outside in the bailey." Mina worried her lower lip between her teeth. "He nodded in greeting."

Ruby's shoulders slumped. How many nights had it been since she conveyed her cryptic message? Three? Four? She lost track of them in her limited capacity as a prisoner within these walls. If her mother received her message, then she could not expect her to arrive at the gates demanding entrance.

She sent Matthew with a warning telling her mother to stay away. Hide. Run if she can. Ruby would have risked a longer message, but with Francis as vigilant in her protection as he was in the destruction of any of his brother's remaining credibility, she could take no chances.

The day after their return, Francis issued a proclamation with a warrant for Crispin's arrest as well as Henry's. Wanted for treason and murder. Regicide. Patricide. The claim itself left Vivienne stunned with disbelief.

Francis played the sainted hero, relaying the confession his brother made under duress on his knees. Ruby heard it with her own ears, but to hear Francis tell the tale, one would think Crispin relished the knowledge he was responsible for his father's death. She knew better. He may be brash and selfish and quick to vengeance, but he would never risk his claim to the throne.

"Will you be wearing your crown?" Mina's question pulled Ruby from her thoughts.

"If you think it suits the occasion." Ruby shrugged. "My apologies, my mind is quite burdened this evening."

Mina rested her hand on Ruby's shoulder. "You need not apologize, my lady." She lifted the gold crown inlaid with rubies and pearls. "This will serve as a reminder for our guests. You are the queen and the daughter of a king."

Ruby trailed her fingers over the jeweled headpiece and

pride infused her. "Very well." If she could not use her words, then she would use her presence to convey a message to the world. Though she may be broken and bruised, she showed resilience and commanded respect due her station.

As Mina pinned it into place, a knock shattered the stillness. Ruby jumped and pressed her hand against her heart to stop it racing. When had she become as nervous as a newborn colt?

Vivienne appeared in the open doorway. "The guests have arrived. We await your presence." Her warm smile nearly destroyed what remained of Ruby's resolve.

Her jaw trembled and tears pricked her eyes. She dropped her gaze before Vivienne could see the overwhelming emotion bubbling up.

"You may go, Mina. Close the door behind you." Vivienne dismissed the young girl.

Ruby's gaze remained fixed on her slippers peeking out from beneath the hem of her skirts. Her heart hung like a lodestone in her chest. The unbearable silence ripped her at the seams. A series of cracks appeared in the well-fortified dam keeping her sobs at bay. She vowed she would not break. She would not cry in front of Vivienne, no matter how much her heart ached and she longed for comfort. If she allowed it, the truth would pour forth unchecked.

Ruby could not risk the safety of her mother, her friend, and her love. She swallowed the anguish and swiped the tears away before Vivienne could see them.

"Are you well?" Crispin's mother tipped her chin up with her fingertips until their gazes met. "My dear, you have been through so much. If you need to speak, then do so. I promise to be impartial and offer only comfort."

"My thanks for your concern." Ruby's voice cracked, and she cursed the show of weakness. There would be a time for grief and healing. But this was the time for decisive action, and unfortunately, she could not drive a wedge between a mother and her sons. At least not until she gained proof of Francis's lies.

"You can trust me, Ruby." Vivienne searched her gaze intently as though trying to convey an unspoken message in the depths of her eyes. Eyes so familiar it caused her physical pain. Crispin's eyes.

"I know." With a nod, Ruby forced a smile.

"If you wish to abstain from making an appearance, I understand completely. I will convey your apologies to Francis and tell him you are indisposed." Vivienne's hands rested on Ruby's shoulders and rubbed gently. "No one would fault you for taking time to rest."

"I am quite capable of attending. The people must see I am hale and hearty in spite of my harrowing experience." She willed the confidence of her words to infuse her spirit, but it whimpered at the thought of being exposed once more.

Vivienne regarded her silently for a long moment. Ruby shifted uncomfortably and fidgeted with the hem of her sleeve. If she persisted, Ruby feared her façade would crack and disintegrate into a thousand pieces.

Finally, a heavy sigh broke the tension. "I cannot force you to do something. Nor would I attempt to do so." Vivienne took Ruby by the arm. "Let us proceed then. The guests await."

And Francis. Ruby bit her tongue to keep from speaking his name aloud.

The guards stepped aside when they ventured into the corridor and fell into step behind them. Ruby glanced over her shoulder, taking note of the men assigned to protect her. She did not know their names, but their faces were familiar to her. They trained with Henry. They had once been loyal to Crispin. Now they followed the desperate orders of a madman.

Ruby braced for the crowd awaiting her. Francis would parade her before them like a prize much as Crispin had once done. But Crispin had been quite open in his desires. Francis put on a farce with his lies and deception. Her stomach churned at the thought of him ruling the kingdom in his brother's place.

When Vivienne led her into the great hall, the room fell silent. A pleasant, friendly smile remained on her lips as her gaze drifted over the guests seated around the room. Courtiers and lords with their placating smiles watched in ignorance as the farce unfurled before them. Upon spying Francis seated in

Crispin's seat at the head table, her smile faltered.

Instinct told her to run as far and as fast as she could. But her feet were rooted to the path set before her.

"You look lovely, my dear." Francis took her hand in his and pressed a kiss upon her fingertips.

Ruby refrained from ripping her hand from his grasp. Bile stung her throat at his touch. Revulsion filled her, festering like a putrid wound. She longed to be away from him but remained mindful of the guests watching them intently.

The members of the privy council sat along the far wall. Families of some of the most prominent houses in the kingdom sat throughout the hall. Their curiosity brought them to see the long-lost prince who had been resurrected from the flames. But Ruby knew they came to see the shame Crispin brought upon his name and his queen.

Keeping her pride clutched tightly to her heart, Ruby acknowledged those in attendance and sat in the vacant chair beside Francis.

He lifted his goblet and raised it high. "To Eleanor, queen of Meradin."

The guests lifted their goblets high in salute and cheered in agreement.

Ruby's face heated at the toast. They knew nothing. Ignorant and self-indulgent, they came only to ensure their place in Francis's kingdom, betraying their loyalty to Crispin. She was a pawn, a tool used to further their purpose and provide something lovely to gaze upon. Her hands clenched in her skirts, even as she demurely dipped her head in humility when they toasted in honor of her.

Francis resumed his seat beside her, but his focus remained on the man to his left, not on her. He seemed as disinterested in her presence as she in his. The knowledge suited her. She detested any interaction with him.

Ruby sipped her wine and took in the scene before her. Many of those in attendance she had met at the feast the night before she was taken. Dread settled through her. How many of them stood beside Crispin when they realized she had been taken by force? She could trust none of them, and it left a bitter taste in her mouth knowing how truly alone she was.

A servant appeared beside her. "More wine, your highness?"

Ruby pushed her goblet toward the servant and swallowed the hopelessness rising from the pit of her stomach. The soft brush of breath against her ear made her blood chill.

"Postern gate. Now," the servant whispered in her ear, and just as quick as it appeared, their presence receded.

Ruby glanced at the woman who retreated. From this angle, she could not see her face, but a growing sense of dread filled her heart.

Waiting a few moments, Ruby pondered the words whispered in haste. Was this her opportunity to escape? A trap? A test of obedience? She bit her lip and tapped her fingers on the goblet. The woman seemed in earnest. Ruby cursed her lack of attention. She should not take direction from an unknown person. In a den of liars and traitors, she could trust no one.

Curiosity fluttered in her chest. She should obey. But if Francis caught her, he would punish Crispin and Henry. How much more punishment could they possibly endure? She could not live with the knowledge her actions caused them harm or even brought their deaths.

Ruby pushed the goblet aside and rose to her feet. "I beg your pardon, your majesty. I crave your indulgence, it seems I am still not fully recovered."

Francis regarded her for a silent moment before rising to his feet and taking her hand in his. "Of course, my dear." His eyes glinted in warning even though his words were silken and sweet like honey.

She slipped from the table and wiped her hand on her dress, wishing she could scrub the skin where he touched her. The two guards fell into step behind her as she wove back through the corridors toward her chamber. How could she slip away from their watchful eye?

When she reached her room, Ruby graced them with a smile and closed the door behind her. Finally alone, she took a deep breath. She struggled with her garments, cursing the laces along the dress and wishing she had summoned Mina to help her disrobe.

After some time wrangling herself from the confines of the dress, Ruby breathed a sigh of relief when it lay in a heap on the floor. She retrieved her hose and tunic from the wardrobe. Whatever lay before her, she wished to be prepared. If she were risking her life and the lives of those she loved, then she needed to give herself the best advantage possible.

Ruby prayed it was not a trap, but she could no longer remain passive beside Francis and pretend. Death would be preferable to being subjected to living with such a fiend.

She pulled on her leather boots and fastened her belt around her waist. The familiar garments lent her a sense of empowerment. If only she had her dagger and bow. Perhaps she could locate a weapon later, first, she had a meeting at the postern gate.

Ruby cracked the door, unsure of how she could slip past her guards. Outside her room, the two guards lay slumped against the wall. She swung the door wide and stared in disbelief at the slumbering guards.

They made no movement when she stepped around them. Their sleep was most unnatural. Then she noticed the empty flask beside them. Perhaps they had been drugged. *The servant. The wine.* Had she slipped a sleeping drought into the wine and offered it to them?

It mattered not. This was her opportunity to slip away unnoticed. Elation drove her to action. With hurried steps, she raced down the staircase leading into the kitchens. With her hood up, Ruby slipped through the servants, hoping none would take notice of her.

When she reached the door leading to the rear of the castle and the postern gate, relief filled her. She was close. So close. Outside, a torch flickered near the gate portcullis and the small arched door.

Keeping to the shadows, Ruby edged along the wall and made her way toward the postern gate. She prayed whatever or whoever waited for her there offered her escape. While she did not know the exact location of the keep where Francis held Crispin and Henry, she could form a plan only if she broke free from Francis's hold. When he discovered her absence, he would send a messenger. Then she could follow them.

A hooded figure waited near the gate. Ruby paused behind a crate, praying it was the person she was meant to meet and not a guard. She crouched lower when a shrill whistle pierced the darkness.

The guard standing by the gate took off at a run, disappearing around the corner. Ruby seized her opportunity and dashed toward freedom. She unlocked the gate and slipped through.

The moment she stepped from the secure fortress, her heart took flight. She was free. Free. Now she could go to them. But where would they go after? She did not know and did not care. All that mattered was saving Crispin and Henry. Then they could do as Marian and Guy had done. They could run away and start over somewhere else. Ruby would rather be happy and an outlaw than a prisoner and a queen.

Determined, Ruby fixed her hood and raced along the wall toward the forest. She collided with something warm and solid. A hand clamped over her mouth, stifling her scream. Panic gripped her with iron jaws as the assailant dragged her into the yawning darkness.

'Twas a trap!

Chapter Eighteen

After having nearly drowned and been subsequently resurrected, Henry counted himself fortunate to have full faculty of his person. However gazing up at the imposing walls surrounding the castle where he was raised, he almost wished he had died. At least it would have offered him some relief. Storming the castle was suicide. He may as well throw himself onto his own sword.

When Crispin realized Francis was hosting a feast in his own honor, he lost all sense of reason. Any caution disappeared in the darkness like a plume of smoke caught up by the slightest breeze. He thought to utilize the confusion inside the castle as a cover to slip inside unnoticed, but Henry found the plan reckless. How in the devil could he enter the castle unnoticed? He was the dethroned king and a wanted traitor.

Henry leaned against the tree. The horses were tied deep in the forest, close enough as to be retrieved quickly but hidden from view of anyone who may pass by. From a hundred yards, Henry could barely see the guards pacing the battlements. From the rear of the keep, torchlight illuminated the postern gate alone. Confused, he resigned himself to the fact Crispin must have an alternative option to breach the inner sanctum and retrieve Ruby.

Shadows played tricks with his vision. Perhaps he was injured worse than he believed. Even though his swollen eye hindered his line of sight, he was still able to use it. He squinted focusing harder on the wall outside the postern gate. A flicker of movement, then nothing.

Perhaps a closer look would serve him better. Careful to remain silent, Henry broke from his post and made his way across the gully at the base of the castle. From this vantage, he could see the postern gate clearly.

One of the guards stumbled through the door and glanced around. He swayed, bracing his hand against the wall. The door stood open behind him.

Henry considered his options. He could remain and wait for Crispin as he promised, or he could attempt to rescue Ruby. Before he could decide, the guard slumped to the ground with a muffled thud.

A hooded figure filled the door. *Crispin.* He rose from hiding and crept closer. The figure spotted him and drew their sword. Henry's gaze rested on the blade. Most definitely not Crispin.

Henry raised his hands knowing he had been caught. How careless could he be? He cursed himself, and dread filled him at the thought of facing Francis on his knees once more.

A shout echoed from inside the wall. The figure rushed toward him, dragging him to the ground in the gully, pinning him down with their full weight.

His breath whooshed from his chest in a rush. The throbbing pain in his head returned as his head struck the ground. Henry lay there, stunned. He gripped the stranger's cloak, bracing for a fight.

"Henry?" The soft, familiar voice fluttered down from the tangled fabric atop him.

He stilled instantly. Every alarm raised in his mind, he pushed himself away, clawing to free himself from her grasp.

The hood fell back, revealing luminous green eyes and chestnut locks.

"Ivy." Her name burned his tongue with revulsion and reverence.

Her hands rested on his arms, pinning him to the ground beneath him. "Quiet."

Henry stilled as the distant sound of voices and footsteps crunching on the dirt. He held Ivy's gaze until the sounds faded once more. She relaxed and released her hold but remained, sitting astride him.

His breath came quicker, not from exertion but from pure need. She betrayed them. She left them for dead. The dueling emotions twisted and writhed like serpents in his chest battling for control. He longed to reach up and stroke her cheek. But the uncontrollable urge to wrap his fingers around her neck and squeeze the life from her enticed him with equal force.

"Forgive me," she whispered. Slowly she slid off him and helped him to his feet. Her gaze shifted to the wall where the gate stood silent and undisturbed. A frown stole across her lips. "Come. We must take cover."

Even though he did not trust her, he took her arm. With her aid, they hobbled back to the forest where he had been watching. He collapsed against the broad oak tree and allowed himself a few moments to recover his wits before facing her.

"What game are you playing, Ivy?" Exhaustion consumed him at the thoughts racing through his mind. A startling realization made his heart still within his chest. "Does Francis know we have escaped?"

Ivy's gaze remained fixed on the postern gate as though she also waited for someone. "Aye, but he does not know I have returned to Culver."

"You betrayed us on several occasions." Henry folded his arms across his chest. "Forgive me if I do not take your word for it."

"Crispin is inside the keep?" Her sidelong glance made his breath hitch. Saints, she was lovely but dangerous, he reminded himself.

Henry could not respond. He feared doing so would only play into her motives, whatever they were. He could no longer trust her, and in his weakened state, overpowering him would take little effort on her part. He rested his hand on the hilt of his sword.

"When your brothers found me inside that cell, they released me thinking my loyalty remained with Francis." Her voice softened. "When they told me you had fallen in the river, I convinced them the river had finished the task they obviously could not."

"You thought we were dead?" Henry arched his brow in surprise.

"I knew you were alive. 'Twould take more than that to kill the two strongest men in Meradin." Ivy reached for him, but Henry ducked away unable and unwilling to let her manipulate him. If he allowed himself to fall under her spell again, he deserved the consequences. She dropped her hand, disappointment curving her plush lips into a frown.

"So you returned to Culver to warn Francis and interfere with our rescue?" Henry scowled, angry both at himself for his body's reaction to Ivy and her for teasing him so effortlessly.

"I have come to aid in your rescue." Her gaze flickered to the postern gate.

Henry scoffed unable to contain his disbelief. "You led us into the trap and delivered us into the hands of the enemy. Why should I believe your lies?"

"Because they are not lies." She exhaled sharply. "The queen and I have a bargain. I will uphold my part in the agreement."

"You betrayed us, revealing our movements to the enemy. Then you led Crispin into an ambush. We were tortured and beaten while you watched," Henry growled. His patience snapped. Closing the gap between them, he gripped her shoulders and pinned her to the oak tree. "Enough lies, Ivy. You had your opportunity to win my trust and my love. And yet you abandoned it at the behest of your *master*." The words left a bitter sting on his tongue.

Ivy did not struggle. She provided no resistance. Her eyes met his, and even in the thick shadows around them, he saw the vulnerability in their depths. She reached up and cupped his cheek. He melted beneath her touch. Biting back a moan, Henry stiffened in an attempt to stave off the overwhelming emotion. He was not strong enough to resist her. He loved her too much.

"Nothing I say will convince you." She stroked his bearded jaw, and he leaned into the touch. "My actions may have led you into Francis's trap, but they have also given you the tools to defeat him should you care to examine them."

Henry released her and stepped back, crushing the overwhelming desire to kiss her. "Why are you here, Ivy? Why were you inside the castle?"

"To save Ruby." Ivy straightened and tugged her cloak back into place. "I delivered instructions for her to meet me at the postern gate." She shook her head. "She returned to her chambers, and I ensured her path to the gate was clear. But something must have happened."

"Perhaps Crispin found her before she could reach the gate?" Henry hoped this was the case, because if it was not, then he could not fathom the horrors Francis would unleash upon her should he catch her attempting to escape his grasp.

The tone of Ivy's voice reflected his thoughts. "If you have not seen her, then someone must have stopped her."

"'Tis possible she slipped out without my notice." Henry feigned confidence even though he held little hope of its validity. "My vision is blurred at this distance, especially in the dark."

Ivy brushed her fingers over his cheek beneath his swollen eye. His heart pounded at the innocent touch. He took her hand in his and brought her fingertips to his lips. Her gasp of surprise set his body aflame.

The snap of a branch behind them jerked him from the intimate moment. Henry drew his sword. Ivy pulled two daggers from her belt. They scanned the dark trees for any movement. He glimpsed the shifting shadows of the horses where they stood tethered, but nothing seemed disturbed otherwise.

Tension and uncertainty wound Henry tight like the string on a longbow. He could no longer sit and wait. Something had happened. Crispin had been captured; he knew it. And if Ivy told the truth, then Ruby had been stopped before she could leave the keep. No one would come to their aid, for there was no one remaining.

He took a deep breath and turned to Ivy. "Can you get us in?"

Ivy nodded, her face solemn. With a well-placed strike, she disarmed him.

Henry sank to his knees in defeat. He could only pray his faith was not misplaced, but as she bound his wrists with leather, he feared he played right into her hands and surrendered to the enemy without a fight.

Chapter Nineteen

The yawning darkness stretched before him. His hand trailed over the damp, cold walls of the long-abandoned tunnel. No one knew of its location save his immediate family, including Francis. He prayed his brother forgot about it in his brush with death.

If he had not forgotten, then Crispin would be walking into a trap. Either way, 'twas the sole entry point available to him. He would be easily recognized if he encountered anyone within the castle walls.

He crept along the corridors, praying it had not collapsed over the years since he last utilized it. Their father once caught them using it as young boys and they were severely chastised. The tunnels' purpose was solely for use in cases of life and death to protect the members of the royal family, which is why they were never allowed to disclose its location to another living soul. Even Henry did not know of its existence.

His fingers tangled in cobwebs as he reached the metal gate. A key. Damn. He forgot it was locked. But he also knew the padlock was old and weak. A few hard strikes with the hilt of his sword, and it broke free. That would certainly need to be replaced, not that it mattered.

The hinges creaked as he opened the metal gate. On the other side, he found a latch built into the wall. With a bit of effort, he shifted it into place. The door swung open under his weight, revealing the dark recesses of the wine cellar built beneath the castle kitchen.

He closed the false wall silently behind him, ensuring it latched completely before using the wall of kegs to lead him to the staircase through the darkness. Armed with his dagger and his sword, he climbed the stairs, being sure to hide his face beneath the deep recesses of his hood.

With his worn, borrowed clothes and scratchy woolen

cloak, no one would look twice at his face. But he smeared ash on it before he entered the tunnel hoping it would mask his features enough should someone catch a glimpse of his profile.

Marian should have had enough time to lure Ruby away from the feast.

When he realized the bastard who stole his throne and his bride intended to celebrate with a feast while smearing his name and reputation in the mud, Crispin could no longer contain his rage. They could not wait for the castle to sleep. Crispin wanted to slit his brother's throat in front of all his guests and show them the true king of Meradin.

He would need to expose his deception first. No reason to martyr the bastard. If he were able to reveal his brother's duplicity, then it would turn the favor of the people back to himself. How could he draw him out? If only he could convince his mother of what he had seen, of what Francis had done to Ruby and Henry, of what he intended to do to his people. His mother still held sway with the privy council and the people of Meradin. Vivienne Saville was above reproach. Even as queen, her opinion often swayed hearts and minds much more effectively than any threats of violence and retaliation. If he could convince his mother, then he could unmask Francis.

Crispin clung to the shadows as he stalked through the corridors careful not to cross paths with any servants or guests who may be wandering. He climbed the stairs toward the raucous sounds of music and laughter. The further he climbed, the louder it became. He reached the small landing, crossing into the small balcony overlooking the great hall. From above he saw the guests among the rows of tables and the head table at the back of the room.

His gaze narrowed on Francis and an overwhelming hatred boiled within him. He would kill his brother for what he did to Ruby, and he would take pleasure in watching the life drain from his eyes as his blood stained his hands and his blade.

Pulling his attention from Francis, he scoured the rest of the head table. Both his mother and Ruby were absent. Perhaps Marian had been able to pull them both away even though her mission was only to draw Ruby away from the festivities and ensure her safety.

Crispin watched for a few moments but finally pulled himself away. His plan to have Marian lure Ruby to the postern gate seemed to have worked. He fully intended to slip out through the kitchen and rendezvous with her there, but his vengeance demanded satisfaction.

His conscience commanded he leave, take her with him and ride until they reached England. There they could make their journey to the continent and live in obscurity until they grew old together and died in each other's arms. But Crispin could not bear the thought of his brother claiming victory. He rested his hand on the dagger at his hip.

A breath caught in his chest at the sight of his mother as she entered the great hall. She sat at the end of the head table, her attention focused on the guests before her and not the imposter to her left. Her wicked son.

If he could somehow get a message to her, he could warn her. But who could he trust? Marian had done her part and escaped with Ruby if all had gone to plan. Why would he linger and risk capture?

A guard approached Francis, leaning down to whisper in his ear. Crispin watched in anticipation. With a nod, his brother pushed away from the table and followed the guard from the great hall. Giddy excitement filled him. If he could confront his brother alone, then he could end this in silence and blame it on a rogue assassin.

As his mind filled in the details, Crispin moved swiftly to follow their path. He remained hidden in doorways and alcoves, following the sound of their heavy footfalls echoing down the hall. They were going to his private chamber.

The thrill of the hunt drew him into a haze. Crispin followed, rounding the corner as the door closed behind his brother. The guard continued down the hallway. Alone. In Crispin's chamber. He could not have asked for a better ambush.

One swipe of his blade, and he could end it. Reclaim his throne and his bride without fear of reprisal. With Ruby and

Henry to testify to his actions, they would have the proof they needed to convince the privy council they acted in defense of the kingdom.

Crispin drew his dagger and silently crossed to the door. He rested his hand on the latch and inhaled deeply, bracing himself for the glory of his *coup de grâce*. The latch turned beneath his hand.

The cold press of steel against his throat turned his molten blood to ice. His blade clattered to the ground and the door swung open.

Francis stood before him, a devilish smile twisting his deformed face into a mask of fiendish horror.

Crispin fought the urge to lunge at him and beat the smirk from his hideous face. The guard gripped his hood and ripped it back, revealing his face completely. Francis's sardonic smile grew even wider.

"How predictable," Francis drawled with obvious delight. "Perhaps I should behead you together." He stepped aside revealing a mass of wool kneeling on the floor.

"Ruby." Her gaze snapped up at the sound of his voice.

"Crispin." Tears streamed down her face, but she held her head high in pure defiance. "Forgive me. I tried to escape." She hiccoughed and the tears fell harder.

"Enough sentiment. Let us take this loving reunion to the great hall and show our guests what happens to traitors to the crown." Francis hauled Ruby to her feet by her arm. Bound by the wrists, she writhed against his hold with no success.

Crispin stepped forward to intervene, but the guard held his arm with one hand while the blade dug into his flesh. The warm trickle of blood revealed the seriousness of the man's intent to use it should he find it necessary.

"Come along." Francis pulled Ruby out of the room and down the corridor.

The guard dragged Crispin along behind them. As they made their way to face judgment before Francis's honored guests, Crispin kept his gaze solely on Ruby. He cursed himself for a fool. Had he retrieved her himself, they could have escaped.

Now they would face his brother's wrath and not even his mother's tearful pleas for mercy could save them. He missed his one opportunity to save them all, and for what, by bowing to his need to sate his hunger for vengeance.

He could not bear to think of Marian or Henry. They were probably killed the moment they resisted. Tortured to gain information and then slaughtered. He could not mourn them for soon he would also meet the same fate. His brother would use them as an example, a warning, to any who defy him or question his rule.

When they reached the great hall, the room fell silent. Crispin felt every eye turn in their direction as Francis dropped Ruby on the floor at his feet.

She rose to her knees and faced him, hatred marring her lovely face.

The guard pushed Crispin to his knees beside her. He longed to reach for her and offer comfort, but when he grasped her hand in his, Francis kicked it away.

A murmur rose through the crowd. Crispin's gaze flickered to his mother who rose to her feet. All the color drained from her cheeks, leaving them ashen and her eyes hollow.

"What is the meaning of his?" Vivienne demanded, rounding the table.

"My brother is an outlaw, a traitor to the crown. He came to steal away my betrothed." Francis's harsh scowl fell upon them. "I must punish them according to the law."

"You lying bastard!" Crispin's shout echoed off the rafters. He attempted to rise, but the guard backhanded him, making his head spin. He collapsed to the floor. When he lifted his head, he spit, and a mouthful of blood stained his brother's boot.

Behind them, the door swung open with a loud bang and shouting filled the room.

Crispin turned to see a group of guards carrying two figures. They dumped the first beside him. *Henry.* Then the other. *Ivy.* Crispin's brow rose in surprise. Before he could say a word, Francis clapped his hands with joy.

A fury unlike any he experienced in his life settled like a

storm cloud around him, engulfing him, raging through his body. An overflowing river hellbent on destroying everything in its path. Francis finally had them exactly where he wanted them. On their knees before the world, awaiting their punishment.

If he thought Crispin would beg to spare his life, he was wrong. Francis would die if he persisted in this farce, and Crispin would welcome death himself if it ensured his brother joined him.

Chapter Twenty

The tension ebbed off Crispin in waves. Ruby stole a glance at him without turning her face away from the vengeful beast claiming to be the rightful heir of Meradin. Her loathing for Francis increased with every moment spent in his company. Her hope of being free of his grasp died the moment the guard seized her outside the gate.

Ruby glared at the imposing man standing to the right of Crispin. The guard straightened after delivering a blow to her husband. He had been the one who captured her. She glared at him, but he remained focused intently on his master. She never wished for her bow or her blade more than in that moment. A smirk played on his lips as his vacant, soulless eyes fixed on her.

Crispin's jaw tensed the moment they dropped Henry behind him. Seeing Ivy carried in against her will along with Henry solidified the dire situation in which they found themselves. There was truly no hope of escape. With every eye trained on them spread prostrate before Francis and no possibility of mercy, hopeless dread settled in the pit of her stomach.

"Distinguished guests, forgive the intrusion." Francis raised his voice to carry across the room. "It seems the prodigal son has returned."

A low murmur rippled through the crowd.

Francis lifted his hands in supplication. "It may come as no surprise to some to discover the truth about my brother, Crispin. His actions over the years have branded him as self-indulgent and hedonistic, earning him the moniker The Prince of Whispers. No one is more stunned than I to uncover the truth behind his selfish actions."

Ruby watched in horror as Francis wove his spell over the masses. The crowd leaned forward in anticipation of his tale. He paced the small space and, with an air of regret and pious humility, lowered his head for a solemn moment of introspection before meeting the voracious crowd's gaze once more.

"It has been revealed that my brother, Crispin, hired an assassin to poison our father. The king." His accusation hung heavily in the air.

A chorus of gasps erupted into a cacophony of chatter. The news shook the foundation of the castle itself as the people absorbed the horror of the implications.

The crowd fell silent as Vivienne stepped forward, her attention focused solely on Crispin. "Is this true?"

Crispin slowly lifted his head and met his mother's stern expression. Ruby's heart ached at the defeat etched upon his features. The confidence he once bore with such effortless grace had been reduced to ash. Stripped bare and thwarted at every turn, Crispin cobbled together what strength remained as he straightened and held her gaze. Ruby's breath lodged in her chest.

"I did not murder my father." Crispin's voice shattered the tense silence.

The crowd burst into a flurry of movement and shouts. Chaos reigned in the aftermath of his response.

Ruby slumped in relief. For a moment, she thought he conceded defeat, but within those words, she heard his refusal to comply with Francis's twisted interpretation of the truth. She watched Vivienne, praying she would see through the deception playing out before them like a mummer's farce.

Vivienne squared her shoulders. Her face softened the smallest fraction before disappearing behind a mask of indifference. Had Francis been watching his mother, he would have seen it. They all would have. Her gaze shifted from Crispin to Ruby.

Without words, she pleaded for aid, hoping the woman she embraced as a friend and a mother would see the shredded remnants of her soul bared before her. Vivienne folded her hands.

"What proof have you of his guilt?" a lone voice rose from

the crowd to her left.

Ruby glanced toward the table where the privy council sat watching the events unfolding before them. Their stoic faces were pinched tight with a mixture of fear, uncertainty, anger, and doubt. But one man stood taller than the rest, his voice raised in curious defiance.

"Does his adamant refusal not reek of fear? Do his past deeds not account for his definitive lack in one's ability instill trust that his words are truthful?" Francis remained calm even though Ruby heard the undercurrent of anger threatening to sweep them beneath the surface of the calm waters of his carefully crafted façade.

"At least I have been faithful to my own nature." Crispin sneered, his tone low and dangerous. "You hide behind false humility and sacrilegious piety. Your lies grow with every breath. I hope you rot in hell for what you have done to me...to my queen."

Tears pricked at her eyes. A sob caught in her throat. He fought for her, even on their knees before their enemy, beaten and bruised, tattered beyond repair, he fought for her honor. Pride swelled inside her chest, filling her heart to bursting. Even if this moment led to their deaths, she knew beyond any doubt Crispin loved her more than he loved himself.

"You stole my queen, tortured her, ripped our child from her womb, and yet you stand before me with the audacity to call me a selfish bastard and a murderer." Crispin bared his teeth. "I should have killed you when I had the chance."

Vivienne gasped, drawing Ruby's attention. Her eyes filled with tears at the sight of Crispin's mother clutching her bodice above her heart, her wide blue eyes filled with sorrow. She wanted to throw herself into her arms and grieve with her.

A loud crack echoed through the room. Crispin fell sideways from the impact of the guard's strike against his head. He collided with Ruby, knocking them both to the ground.

Before she could speak, the guard hauled Crispin back to his knees and held a blade to his throat. Blood ran from his nose, staining the front of his tunic.

"The next time you speak to the king in such a manner, I will cut out your tongue." The guard hissed, his voice so low Ruby nearly missed the exchange.

Her eyes widened with horror knowing he would do much worse than that if given the opportunity and the permission. She righted herself, casting a cautious glance around the room. The guests seemed equally as stunned and horrified by the confrontation before them. Even the privy council sat quietly as though weighing the outcome in their mind and debating on the wisdom of interjecting further. This quarrel, it seemed, lay between the brothers, and no one wished to be caught in the maelstrom of their anger.

"His desperation knows no bounds," Francis lamented with a frown. He drew Vivienne closer, allowing her to stand by his side and stare down at Crispin. The pressure of his hand on her arm belied her unwillingness to be drawn into the center of their battle.

"He knows nothing of ruling a county. Indulging in wine and women, whoring his way through the kingdom," Francis continued, spinning his web of deceit. "Even Henry, his companion, has been seduced by his hedonism. They share everything. Even the queen."

Ruby's face heated, but she refused to be shamed by his words. Holding her ground, she ignored the whispers around them.

"After years of lies and secrecy, is it truly so difficult to believe he would threaten me with falsehoods and use his closest companion to play a role in his selfish desires?" A wickedness consumed him as he spoke. "He took the queen to place the blame upon me. To keep me from taking the throne as I am rightfully able to do, even after I returned to the monastery content to live my days in the service of the Lord."

She nearly vomited at the brazen lies spilling from his twisted mouth.

"I offered my support, my companionship, and my trust." Francis pressed his hand to his chest. "And he betrayed me, casting me into the flames and threatening my life should I not comply with his demands. He longed to portray me as the villain when he himself fills the role without hesitation."

"You damned liar!" Henry shouted from behind them. He sprang to his feet, pushing through Crispin and Ruby, lunging directly for Francis.

Vivienne stumbled away as Francis stepped out of reach. Henry came to a stop an arm's length from Francis, his hands outstretched when he collapsed in a heap clutching his side. Ruby reached for him, rolling him onto his back. Her hands slipped in the blood pouring from the gash across his torso. It spilled over the stone beneath him, spreading like a blanket of red across the white stone.

A scream wrenched from her throat.

The world dimmed around her as she turned to face the guard wielding his blade slick and dripping with Henry's blood. Crispin attempted to move, but the blade resumed its position against his throat.

"Henry!" Ivy scrambled forward, cradling Henry's head in her lap. His groans filled the air, casting a somber silence across the crowd.

"Take him away." Francis waved his hand to the guards standing behind them. "Let him die elsewhere."

The guards lifted Henry, pulling him from Ivy and Ruby's relentless grip. They dragged him from the great hall and out into the bailey.

A cry of protest rose from the guests. They obviously did not agree with Francis's blatant dismissal of Henry's life. Ruby turned to the privy council ready to demand their intercession in stopping the madness.

"Silence!" Francis shouted. "The traitor deserves a traitor's death. His attack on me was unprovoked and unwarranted. I have every right to defend myself. As a king does."

"You are no king," Crispin spat, his face contorted with rage. "A king would not kill an unarmed man."

"Henry Balmont was a traitor. As are you." He turned and held Ruby's gaze. "And even you, sweeting."

Disgust left a bitter taste in her mouth. Plunging a blade

into his chest and ripping out his heart would be worth the punishment of treason. If only she had a weapon...

"There are most certainly traitors in our midst." Vivienne stepped forward, her gaze resting on each of them individually before coming to Francis. She rested a hand on his arm. "Thank you for bringing them to our attention."

Francis's smug smile twisted the soured fear in her gut until it gnawed a hole inside her.

Vivienne released Francis and stepped back. "Arrest this man. He is not my son; he is an imposter."

Shouts and screams echoed through the room as the congregation burst into chaos.

Chapter Twenty-One

Crispin's rage transformed into disbelief with those words. He surged to his feet as his trusted guards charged through the doors, surrounding Francis and the handful of men loyal to him.

Shouts and cries of outrage from the guests invited to celebrate Francis's return encircled him. They certainly had not anticipated such an eventful evening. Seizing his opportunity, he ripped the blade from the grip of the guard who stabbed Henry.

"Silence!" His shout boomed over the cacophony. Crispin's gaze skimmed over the crowd. He noted the horrified expressions of the privy council and the tear-stained faces of Ruby and Ivy who sat on the ground staring up at him.

He offered his hand to Ruby who took it and rose to her feet. The noise around them faded into hushed murmurs and shuffling feet as those in the back attempted to gain a better view.

With Ruby by his side, Crispin was renewed. He rounded on his brother, lifting the blade and pointing it at his heart. Two guards flanked the scarred imposter, his arms taken in their iron grips. Francis stood mute between them. Crispin's gaze remained fixed on his adversary.

"Mother, I believe we deserve an explanation for your statement."

"This man who claims to be my eldest son, Francis, is nothing more than a wicked imposter." Vivienne's voice carried across the room. She spoke with clarity and conviction. Not a soul would dare contradict her. Her regal bearing and longstanding position left her with a flawless reputation. She was beyond criticism, and every person in attendance knew it.

"How did you come to this realization?" Crispin asked, his confidence growing with every breath. Ruby's presence beside him bolstered his courage.

"From the beginning, I sensed something different in him.

He claimed to be my son, however he could not remember things my son would easily recall. At first, I thought it was the injury from the fire which stole his memories, but the more he spoke, the less convinced I was of his sincerity." Vivienne came alongside Crispin to face Francis. "He may resemble my son, but his scars hid enough of the difference to shield his true identity and allow us to reconstruct the memory of Francis to fill in the missing pieces."

Vivienne's words vindicated Crispin, but they also surprised him. He never anticipated this man to be an imposter. He merely assumed the fire affected his mind, twisting and warping it into the devious villain who stood before him.

"You knew my son well." She spoke directly to Francis, as though attempting to lure him into a confession. But he stood tall, watching her with a shrewd glare. "But not well enough it seems."

Crispin's mind churned at the possibilities. Who could have possibly known Francis and resembled him close enough to convince the whole of Meradin that he was the golden prince returned from the dead?

"From our first conversation, I harbored my doubts as to his claim. Francis, while not a pious man, was a good man. 'Tis true, God works in mysterious ways, but had he truly been my son, he would have returned the moment he realized the truth of his birth." Vivienne's gaze narrowed. "But 'twas when he returned with Ruby claiming Crispin had turned on him. I knew beyond a doubt he was not the man he claimed to be."

Vivienne turned to Crispin and cupped his cheek. "You may have had your differences, but your brother loved you. He wanted you to succeed and prosper. He would never have branded you a traitor or stolen that which you so obviously treasure."

Crispin swallowed the rising emotion and instead embraced the implication of her words. Francis was never his enemy. His brother loved him. A world of regret threatened to pull him deep into a sea of misery, but he fought against the tide and focused it into the rage burning hot beneath his skin.

"Then who would?" He pressed the tip of the blade to Francis's throat. "Your name, villain, before I end your miserable life."

Wicked laughter bubbled up from the imposter's throat. His eyes grew manic and wild as the laughter consumed him. The scarred flesh around his mouth pulled tight. Then Crispin saw it.

"Simon." There was no question in his mind. How had he completely missed it before? He had been so convinced this scarred bastard was his brother, it never occurred to him that it could be anyone else.

"Did you miss me, Crispin?" Simon sneered. Gone was the meek and humble scarred monk playing king. A monster rose from behind the familiar mask.

"But we thought you died in the fire that night." Crispin shook his head to free the last remaining doubts in his mind. Then it all fell into place. They had been trapped together. Everyone assumed they perished together. Memories slid into place connecting the actions of then to what was unfolding now. Crispin hissed in a breath. "You left him to die."

Simon scoffed, ignoring the press of the blade against his skin. "I dragged him to safety but 'twas too late. By the time the monks found us, Francis was already dead, burned beyond recognition. I barely survived."

Crispin ignored the murmurs rising from the crowd. "So you lied to the monks who saved you."

"I did what I had to do." Simon's smirk grew. "I could not return to the castle. Not when such a prime opportunity lay like a banquet before me. So I recovered in secret and used my time to wait for you to whore your way into an early grave. But when I stumbled across you drunk and bitter, begging for someone to kill your father, I knew my time had finally come."

"You son of a bitch." Crispin poised himself ready to finish Simon with a single stroke of his sword.

"You wanted him dead, and you offered gold coin to ensure it happened. I know, because I was there. I took that coin and purchased what I needed to bring my plan to fruition." His laughter grated against Crispin's restraint.

"God's blood, teeth, and bones! I was angry and my pride injured. We were not on the best of terms, but I did not want him dead!" His hand trembled on the hilt as the consequences of his rash, impulsive actions came to light.

"I needed him dead, and then I needed you to fail spectacularly." Simon's gaze shifted to Ruby. "But I never anticipated her."

Crispin stepped between them, shielding her from Simon's view. "I should kill you for what you have done to her alone. You deserve a fate worse than death for the misery she has endured at your hand."

"I could not have asked for a more perfect opportunity. When I realized she harbored such conflicted emotions for you, how could I not use such knowledge to my benefit?" He chuckled as though divine providence had graced him with such a blessing.

Simon did not need to reveal every detail of his twisted plot. Crispin saw the pieces slowly come together in his mind. From their time training together to their current situation, knowing Simon was at the core of the scheme made much more sense. Simon always harbored a deep-seated loathing for the court because of his standing as a bastard son of a prestigious lord.

"Why?" Ruby's question startled him. She stepped from behind Crispin and faced the man who lied to her, tormented and betrayed her. Crispin's grip on the sword tightened in case the bastard attempted to harm her.

"'Tis what I am owed," Simon hissed, vehemence resounding in his biting words.

"You are owed nothing. Not even mercy." Ruby held his gaze steadily. Pride filled Crispin at her strength. Her voice dropped low. "I once trusted you, but now I know how Eve felt in the garden of Eden. May you burn in hell for the pain you caused. For the lives you took." She turned away in disgust.

As Crispin drew back the sword to deliver a killing stroke, Ruby's hand gripped his arm. Their eyes met, and he saw the heartache in their depths. He lowered his sword to his side.

"Take him away." Crispin conceded with a wave of his

hand. He wrapped a protective arm around Ruby and watched as the guards dragged Simon and his men from the great hall.

A tug on his tunic, and Crispin found himself in a passionate embrace. Ruby's lips held his, drawing him into a kiss so tender it brought tears to his eyes. He nearly lost her, and the thought of such a gem being shattered at the hands of such a monster left him adrift in the darkness. But her touch, her kiss brought him into the light. Hope blossomed in his heart once more.

Cheers and applause filled the great hall. Crispin reluctantly broke the kiss and lifted his hand in acknowledgment of his people. His gaze came to rest on his mother, whose joyful tears spilled across her cheeks. She cupped his face and embraced them both.

Crispin breathed deep savoring this moment of victory. He lost so much to reach this point. If it had not been for his mother, Simon would have fooled the whole kingdom. He owed her a debt of gratitude, as well as an explanation. But that could wait.

Henry. Where was Henry?

As if sensing his concern, Ruby nudged him in the side and pointed to the door where Marian stood wearing a somber expression. The night was far from over. Grief settled around his heart and drew him into the darkness once more. He may have secured the kingdom against an imposter, but he lost the one person aside from Ruby whom he loved beyond measure.

Regret would haunt him until his dying day.

Chapter Twenty-Two

Once Crispin ensured Ruby was safely returned to her chambers, he returned to the great hall determined to ease the tensions the events of the evening brought to a pinnacle. His assurances left her confident he had the matter well in hand. However, her conscience pricked at leaving him to address these issues alone.

She needed rest. 'Twas as if the tension of being pulled toward Francis against her will released and the exhaustion claimed her. He placed a tender kiss on her forehead and instructed her to sleep.

Ruby had not slept comfortably in over a fortnight. Her body surrendered to the blissful embrace of slumber the moment she settled on the bed.

The next morning when Mina came to her chamber, Crispin's continued absence surprised her. She expected him to return sometime during the morn, but as it neared midday, he never arrived. Ruby dressed quickly and sighed with delight at finding her dagger and sheath among her garments. She fastened the belt securely around her hips before leaving her chamber.

Upon reaching Crispin's private chamber, Ruby paused outside the door her hand poised mid-knock. She did not wish to wake him, but she longed to know what transpired once she was taken away to rest. There had been no update on Henry or her mother. Perhaps she should seek out Vivienne first.

The door opened beneath her hand making her jump. Ruby pressed her hand to her chest, quelling the racing of her heart. 'Twas difficult to remind herself Francis was no longer a threat.

"My darling gem." Marian rushed through the doorway and wrapped her arms around her. The loving embrace made her eyes fill with tears. She clung tightly to her mother.

"What are you doing in Crispin's chamber?" Ruby asked,

disentangling herself from her mother's firm hold.

Marian pursed her lips and stepped aside, allowing Ruby to enter the chamber. Vivienne rose to her feet and nodded from the far side of the room. As she approached the bed, fear plunged a dagger into her breast. Had something happened while she slept?

In Crispin's bed, she found Henry. His pale cheeks bore dark blotches, a combination of the bruises and cuts. His left eye was swollen and red. He did not wake when she approached. Tears fell freely, dripping on her bodice.

"Is he dead?" Ruby reached out and touched his hand. Warmth met her touch revitalizing a smidgen of hope in her soul.

"Not yet."

Ruby glanced up to find Ivy seated at the edge of the bed, her hand resting on the blankets beside Henry. Her reddened eyes belied the state of her heart. She loved Henry. Wept for him. Nearly died for him. Even through her betrayal, Ivy's heart belonged to Henry. A member of the Guild bound to a peer of Meradin.

"I should have killed that bastard when I had the chance." Ivy's low voice seethed with regret and anger.

"There are many regrets, but there is naught we can do to alter the past." Ruby joined Ivy on the far side of the bed and rested her hand on the woman's shoulder. Ivy placed her hand on Ruby's and squeezed in acknowledgment.

Marian resumed her position beside the bed where Ruby had stood. She retrieved a mortar and pestle from the table beside the bed. "I have given him a sleeping drought to rest and allow him to heal. The blade struck deep, but only time will tell if he survives or not." Her caring gaze rested upon the injured knight. "He is strong. I have hope."

"Grammercy, Mother." Ruby watched as she placed a poultice on the swollen eye and the varying cuts marring his face.

"Tell me when he wakes," she murmured to Ivy, who nodded, before stepping away.

Vivienne waited by the door. She drew Ruby into a warm embrace. "Crispin is in his presence chamber. He needs you."

She cupped her cheek before pressing a tender kiss upon her brow. "Go to him."

Ruby left knowing Henry was in the best of care. Her mother was a skilled healer. Vivienne and Ivy would ensure Henry got the rest he needed under Marian's skilled attention.

She ventured down the corridor, mindful of the silence engulfing the castle. The distinct lack of servants bustling through the halls was a somber reminder of the traumatic events the night before. Once she reached his presence chamber, she opened the door cautiously.

Crispin lay slumped over his ornate desk, his gentle snores filling the room.

Slowly, she closed the door behind her and crept to where he lay asleep. His hair lay in tousled waves across his forehead. His jaw shadowed with a beard. His dark lashes rested delicately against his pale cheek.

In repose, Crispin instead resembled a younger, more innocent version of himself. Ruby's heart nearly burst with affection at the sight. How she wished she could have known the boy he once was before the harsh realities of royal life fell upon his broad shoulders.

Ruby leaned closer, tracing her fingertips along his forehead, and pushing back the lock of hair. She brushed a cut along his hairline, and he shifted, furrowing his brow at the sensation. When his eyes opened, she lost herself in their crystalline blue depths. He lured her in with a simple look. This was Crispin's gift, his natural ability to disarm someone with a single glance or a tempting smile. But in this moment, there was no barrier between them. Nothing but raw, urgent relief followed by a brilliant flash, and the blazing passion ignited once more.

A lazy smile curled his lips as he lifted his head. Without a word, he drew her across his lap and wrapped his arms around her. She melted into his embrace soaking up the warmth and strength she longed for during their time apart. 'Twas the one thing that kept her sane while locked in the ostentatious room Francis assured her was not a prison. She shivered and Crispin's grip tightened.

"Saints above, I thought I lost you." Crispin buried his face in her hair, inhaling deeply and pressing soft kisses along her forehead.

Ruby tilted her head back and searched his face. She cupped his bearded cheek and smiled, her heart aching from the overabundance of emotion choking her. "I thought the same."

Crispin kissed her with reverence. She fisted her hand in his tunic and clung to him desperate to savor the feel of his body pressed against her, the taste of his lips. They were one, united and bound together for eternity, and nothing could tear them apart.

When she finally broke the kiss, Crispin groaned with obvious disappointment. His cock pressed insistently against her hip. Soon she would have all of him, and they would begin anew. But first, they must face the harsh realities of a kingdom torn asunder by the actions of a malicious imposter.

"I have seen Henry," Ruby spoke carefully, unsure of how Crispin would respond to the report.

As she anticipated, regret and anger clouded Crispin's clear blue gaze creating a storm in their depths. "Is he...?" He could not even bring himself to voice the thought aloud.

"He is resting. My mother is tending to him, along with your mother and Ivy." She smiled in an attempt to bolster hope, but Crispin seemed lost in thought. Ruby rested her hand on his chest. "He is strong. He will recover. I have not abandoned hope."

Crispin's brow furrowed, and he shook his head. "I have failed him. 'Tis as if I thrust the blade into his side myself."

Ruby gripped his jaw in her hand and forced him to meet her gaze. "He acted in your defense. His sole responsibility is to protect the king, and his actions reflected his fealty to the crown." Her voice softened. "You cannot punish yourself. Henry knew the risks and embraced them with honor."

He searched her face and relaxed beneath her touch. "You are as wise as you are beautiful."

The compliment made her cheeks warm. She pushed aside the flattery and instead chose to focus on the questions burning in her mind. "How did you find me?"

Crispin eased back in the chair, settling into a more comfortable position and shifting her firmly against his chest. "Ivy."

Ruby listened intently as Crispin recounted the story of how he found Ivy in his chambers, how she drugged him, their agreement and subsequent journey to place a message in the old tree, and the time spent in the forest waiting. She held her tongue for the duration of the tale, unwilling to spoil the moment, but also taking note of Ivy's behavior. His revelation of her betrayal came as no surprise.

"It seems Ivy played both sides perfectly." Crispin stroked his jaw thoughtfully. "I believe there is more to this tale. Perhaps we should speak to her and then decide what course to take."

"Are you truly the same man?" Ruby stared at him in disbelief. "When I first met you, I believe you were quicker to action than explanation."

"I will not lie, my first impulse is to lock her in the cell beside Francis in the dungeon." He shrugged. "But there is more to this than we can see, and I am intrigued by her commitment to her cause, whatever that may be."

Ruby stared in bewilderment. "Who are you and what have you done with the infamous Prince of Whispers?"

A wicked smirk played upon his lips making her insides melt. "Oh, my sweetling, a man cannot change who he is, but he can transform into something greater." He kissed her neck, making her shiver against him. "My whispers are for you, and you alone. If you wish me to play the villain, your will is my command."

"Crispin." His name graced her lips with a breathy moan. She placed her hand against his chest to stop the riot of need from consuming her completely. He paused and rested his head against hers.

"My apologies, darling." He nuzzled against her neck. "Having you in my arms again awakens the beast within me."

She whimpered at his confession and cleared her throat. "What is to be done about Simon?"

Crispin's ardor cooled as he leaned back against the chair, putting some space between them. "I shall meet with the privy council and discuss his fate. But after such a public revelation, they cannot deny the coup he attempted on the throne." He plucked at the fabric of her gown. "A public execution would be too merciful. He must suffer as we have."

Ruby pondered silently, unable to find the words to argue in defense of the monster who ripped so much joy from her life. Crispin placed his hand over hers and intertwined their fingers.

"Do you still wish to remain my queen?" His somber question cut through the haze of the thoughts crowding her mind.

Her gaze snapped to his. "Why would you ask such a question?"

"After everything you have endured at my hand." He licked his lips and for a brief moment, she saw the vulnerability she glimpsed when he slept. "Do you still wish to be bound to me?"

"Of course, I do." She wrapped her arms around his neck.

"Even after what Francis did to you to subvert me?" Crispin's throat worked as though suppressing the emotions. "He stole our child from your womb. He tortured you. Threatened you. And all to undermine me. To make me suffer."

Ruby inhaled deeply before answering. "You are not responsible for the actions of a madman." She held his gaze and poured her soul into the words, hoping she could steal any doubt from his mind. "I will grieve the loss of this child, but it does not change how I feel about you. I love you, Crispin, and we have the rest of our lives to fill our home with children and laughter and love."

He pulled her close and kissed her. Passion and love drove away any lingering hesitation from her mind. He believed her. They survived, and their future lay bright ahead. When the kiss ended, they were both winded.

"I love you, Ruby." He rested his forehead on hers. "And I will spend the rest of my days showing you exactly how much I treasure you."

"Good." Ruby nestled closer against him delighted to be in

his possession once more. "I shall spend the rest of my days reminding you of that vow."

Chapter Twenty-Three

He must be dead, and yet the excruciating pain shooting down his side revealed him to be very much alive. Henry's eyes ached with the effort of trying to open them. He blinked against the sunlight coming in through the large window.

Light settled around the furniture in the room, bringing the furniture into focus as his gaze sharpened. Rich tapestries, silks and velvets, dark elegantly carved woodwork in the chairs and wardrobes. Henry shifted uncomfortably. This was certainly not his chamber.

His hands fisted in the coverlet. Perhaps he had died. Then he glimpsed the dark curls sprawled across the bed and the woman slumped over the side. Hours of vigilance taken beside his sickbed had rendered her exhausted.

Oh, sweet, deceitful Ivy. His hand felt as though he lifted a horse in his palm, but he persisted for he longed to touch her. He sighed with relief when she did not disappear like a dream on the morning mist. She was real. He was not dead. That knowledge alone left him with hope.

She stirred when he threaded his fingers through her hair. Her lips parted, curving into a bewitching smile. Henry studied her for a long moment. How could he let her go? After all she had done, he still loved her and such sentiment defied logic, even reason. He exhaled sharply at the twisting pain in his side.

When he groaned, her eyes fluttered open. A spark lit in their depths. She smiled and lifted her head to gaze down at him.

"Too stubborn to die." She grinned and took his hand between hers. "I knew as much."

Henry chuckled, and the action sent a bolt of agony through his side. "Do not make me laugh." His hoarse voice cracked from disuse.

Ivy retrieved a small cup from the table beside the bed and

held it to his lips. "Drink this."

Before he could protest, Ivy poured it into his mouth. The sweet, cool liquid quenched the thirst he had not realized until he tasted it. He drank the contents and settled back upon the bed once more, licking his lips.

"What was that?" he asked, his voice stronger. His mind slowly cleared.

"An herbal tea." Ivy set the cup aside and took his hand once more. "Marian left it with strict instructions for you to drink it upon waking."

Marian. Ruby. Crispin. The memories came hurtling toward him like a barrage of arrows striking different parts of him with equal damage. He attempted to sit up, but the motion left him breathless and panting.

Ivy placed her hands firmly on his shoulders pinning him to the bed. "God's blood, Henry. You nearly died. You are in no condition to leave this bed."

He collapsed against the soft bedding and took several deep breaths. When the pain subsided, Henry nodded.

Ivy released him and resumed her seat. "I have been left with strict orders on how to care for you. If I fail, then they truly will have my head."

"What—" Henry paused, unsure if he wanted to know the outcome, but he pushed through the hesitation "What happened after I—?"

"After you threw yourself on the guard's blade?" Ivy's disappointment etched the lines around her mouth.

"I did nothing more than what is expected of me," Henry growled. "My mission is to protect the king and queen without concern for my own well-being."

"Sacrificing yourself does not protect anyone, Henry." She scowled. He wanted to smooth the frown from her lovely lips with his own. After a tense silence, Ivy conceded. "They dragged you from the room to leave you for dead. Then chaos descended like a vengeful storm tearing at the fabric of the kingdom."

"What of Crispin? Ruby?" Fear wrapped around his heart constricting it in its fist.

"The king and queen are quite well," Ivy assured him. "The imposter has been dealt with accordingly."

"The imposter?" Henry shook his head with confusion.

"'Twas not Francis." Crispin's voice filled the void. "My brother is truly dead."

Henry turned to search for his friend and found him leaning against the bedpost watching them. His gaze, so shrewd, softened with obvious relief.

"I am pleased to see you escaped the same fate, Henry. I cannot say I would be able to rule quite as efficiently without you by my side." Crispin sat on the bed beside him.

"You have a strong queen by your side to serve as your conscience in my stead." Henry smiled. "I am certain you would have managed quite well without me."

A flash of sorrow marred Crispin's strong features for only a moment before vanishing. He shook his head. "Thankfully, I will not have to do so."

"I should fetch some water." Ivy backed away from the bed, but Crispin held his hand up, making her pause.

"Stay." He gestured to the seat she occupied earlier.

Ivy settled into the chair with her hands in her lap. Henry reached out his hand, and she laced their fingers together. Her presence warmed him.

"The imposter posing as my brother," Crispin spoke slowly, "'twas Simon."

Henry gasped at the revelation. "How in the devil? He survived? But how? Why?" An onslaught of questions bombarded him. Before he could formulate them into words, Crispin continued recounting the gaps in the story after Henry was wounded and left for dead out in the bailey.

With rapt attention, Henry listened, unsure of what to believe. The tale seemed almost too fantastical. Simon assuming Francis's identity. Using his connections to form an alliance against Crispin. Waiting until Crispin aligned himself perfectly for failure and preying on his flaws.

"Why would Simon do this?" Henry finally asked once Crispin finished his tale.

"You remember Simon so little?" Crispin shook his head. "The arrogance. He believed himself to be the heir to his father's estate, but as a bastard, he could never hold a title. He had to earn it, and when that failed, he resorted to treason."

"All those years training together, I never had reason to doubt his loyalty even though there were whispers of his smuggling activities." Henry could not fathom allowing hatred and greed to fester to such a point.

"None of us did. Which is why I never considered him to be anything other than who he claimed to be." Crispin ran his hand over his clean-shaven jaw.

"How did you know he was not who he claimed?" Henry attempted to work it out in his mind, but there was nothing to lead him to a firm conclusion one way or another.

"My mother discovered the truth." Crispin chuckled. "She is wiser than the rest of us by far."

"They say a mother's intuition is keen," Henry agreed. "What have you done with Simon?"

"He is occupying the dungeon alone with those loyal to him. They will stand trial for their crimes and be punished according to the law of Meradin." Crispin folded his arms across his chest.

Henry stared in surprise. How could this be the same man he held dearer than a brother? Crispin would have taken vengeance into his own hands and wrought destruction upon any who dare cross him. Yet the actions he chose against these traitors bore the hallmark of a true king. Wisdom in leadership comes from ensuring the needs of the many come before one's own selfish desires. Perhaps Crispin would make a fine king after all. As if Henry had ever doubted it.

"There is one who still remains accountable for their part in Simon's sinister plot." Crispin's gaze rested on Ivy.

Henry squeezed her hand, but Ivy remained impassive. She tilted her chin up and met Crispin's accusative stare directly.

"Tell me the truth, Ivy, and I will spare your life." Crispin's words echoed like a death knell in Henry's head. "Are you loyal to the Guild or your masters?"

"I was, but no longer." Ivy's response echoed with conviction.

"When you led me into the forest to place a message in the old oak tree, to whom were you loyal?" Crispin's question lingered without a reply.

A multitude of emotions flickered across Ivy's beautiful face. Finally, she spoke. "The queen."

"Then 'tis safe to assume after this moment your actions were only in the service of the queen and no other."

Ivy nodded firmly.

"You provided us with the location of his fortress by leading us into capture and facilitated our escape when there would have been no opportunity."

As Crispin unraveled Ivy's role, Henry saw the threads connecting in a larger, more intricate pattern. When they assumed she had betrayed them, she had merely provided them with opportunity without revealing her own deviation.

"When you pledged your loyalty to the queen, you meant it." Henry viewed her in an entirely new light. Gone were the malicious actions replaced with strategically provided pieces of information for them to uncover the truth of Simon's plot.

"If I revealed my true intent, he would have killed me without hesitation. I was nothing more than a weapon for him to use and discard as he saw fit." Ivy blinked back the tears forming at the corner of her eyes. "I regret not being able to do more to spare the pain my actions caused both you and the queen."

"I did not know members of the Guild bore a conscience." Crispin's sardonic comment drew her ire.

"I was not a member by choice. I was sold to the Guild and beaten to instill fear and respect for the Guild masters." She narrowed her gaze. "When they sold me to him, I did what I must to survive, hoping to earn my freedom. But the queen showed me mercy and offered me a different path."

Henry smoothed his thumb over her fingertips in an effort to soothe her. He wished he could pull her into his embrace and hold her against his heart. But Crispin was the king and his judgment in this matter superseded Henry's emotional ties to Ivy. He needed to trust his king's decision.

Crispin and Ivy remained locked in a wordless battle for several tense moments before Crispin nodded. "Very well." He turned to Henry. "Do you bear the responsibility for this woman?"

"Of course I do." The affirmation fell from his mouth without consideration, but he could not argue with it. He loved her, beyond reason and understanding.

"Henry." Her sinful voice drew his attention. Their gazes locked.

"I cannot deny the love I have for you, Ivy. While I respect my king and country and vow to serve them in all ways, my heart belongs to you alone."

"As mine belongs to you." Tears broke free, marking her cheeks. She wiped them away with her free hand and smiled.

"From this moment forward, I hold you responsible for this woman. I doubt she will be a meek bride, but somehow I feel you both are well-suited for each other. I shall leave you to recover." After several paces, Crispin turned. "Although, I will be having you moved to another chamber. I cannot have you commandeering my chambers indefinitely." With a smile, he left them in peace.

Ivy sank onto the bed beside Henry. She leaned over him and placed a tender kiss on his lips.

"I love you, Henry. From the first night I saw you, I wanted nothing but you." Her words and the smile on her lips infused him with hope and pride. "I regret deceiving you. From this moment forward, I vow it will never happen again."

"I should hope not." Henry glanced at the door then back at Ivy. "I doubt he will be gracious enough to pardon you a second time."

"Would you?" Ivy cupped his face, and the warmth of her touch sent a bolt of need through him.

"I showed you mercy before, but make no mistake, when you are mine, wholly completely, unequivocally, then I will ensure your loyalty remains steadfast." He wrapped his hand around the back of her neck and held tight, their lips a breath apart. "You will belong to me, body and soul, and there will be no man alive who will possess you as I do."

Ivy whimpered before kissing him. He basked in the sensation of her lips and the sweet taste of her tongue. Even though his body protested, he held her tight against him and claimed what she offered. When he groaned in discomfort, she drew back.

"You should rest." She tried to pull away, but he held her tight.

"Lie with me a while." He lifted his arm and allowed her to lie against his uninjured side. Henry pressed a soft kiss to her head and closed his eyes.

Henry knew not what the future held, but he would savor every moment from this day forward. He might not be dead, but to him, he was certainly in heaven.

Chapter Twenty-Four

Confident in his friend's recovery from his multiple near-death encounters, Crispin ventured from his chamber, allowing Henry and Ivy to discuss this fresh, new beginning. He hoped he had not misplaced his trust in pardoning Ivy and allowing her to remain in his kingdom. After a lengthy conversation with his bride and confirming certain details of her role in Simon's coup, he found himself loathe to allow her to remain within his kingdom, but he could not argue against her affection for Henry or her loyalty to Ruby. She had ample opportunity to make her escape to safety, and yet she chose to remain by Henry's side and even went as far as to aid their escape from the dungeon where Simon left them to rot.

He ventured to the one spot where he knew he would find his mother. The king's private garden. Over the past few days, he neglected to seek her out. Shame filled him for being such a pitiful son. Had he been Francis, the true Francis, he would have sought an audience with her sooner. Much sooner. The truth was, he dreaded the thought of facing her after Simon revealed the truth of his actions concerning the assassination of his father.

Crispin paused outside the garden and took a deep, fortifying breath. He faced the privy council, Henry, a horde of angry villagers, and the confused guests who left in shock after the feast. He could certainly face his own mother. Only a few nights had passed, and yet the whole kingdom was alight with the tale of Simon's duplicity and Crispin's near demise. To their benefit, they did not paint Crispin the hero of the hour, alas, that honor was bestowed upon the rightful bearer. His mother, the lioness of Meradin.

When he stepped into the garden and closed the door behind him, the chill of the approaching winter months burrowed beneath the layers of fabric. He rounded the small alcove and found her sitting on the stone bench wrapped in a wool cloak and cradling a mug of steaming herbal tea in her hands. She glanced up at his appearance and smiled. Her kind eyes warmed him instantly.

"Crispin, join me." She slid to the right and patted the stone bench beside her. "We have much to discuss."

He nodded and took the offered seat. Words failed him. How could he face her? In the midst of it all, she never lost sight of who she was and her dedication to the people of Meradin. He failed her in so many ways, and yet she still welcomed him with open arms and unconditional love.

"You met with the privy council this morning?" She sipped her tea.

"Aye," Crispin replied with a nod. "They have agreed to forgo a trial considering Simon's public confession."

"I am pleased to hear it. Delaying the inevitable will only prolong the work we must do to heal the kingdom." A note of relief painted her words.

Crispin relaxed as the conversation continued. "After I told them of his actions toward Henry and Ruby, they have given me complete authority in selecting his punishment."

His mother searched his face for a long moment without speaking before heaving a heavy sigh. "'Tis your right. What Simon inflicted upon Henry was cruel, but..." She bit her lip when a sob escaped. Tears filled her eyes. "To have your child ripped from your body in such a manner...I cannot imagine the agony Ruby endured. My heart aches for her." Her hand rested over her heart, and her gaze focused on the angel statue amid the barren rose bushes.

"Simon will pay for his cruelty and for the suffering he inflicted with such obvious pleasure." Crispin sneered, his passion overruled any sensible control he possessed. "I will ensure he receives a punishment befitting his crimes."

"Forgive me for not speaking of my doubts sooner, but 'twas not until Ruby returned with Simon I knew without question he was not my son." She reached out and cupped Crispin's cheek in her hand. "Francis was a kind soul and a gentle man. He would never have acted against you in such a manner."

Crispin bristled at the praise she foisted upon his deceased brother. "Ah yes, the golden prince. A martyr for the kingdom of Meradin." Scorn laced his voice, but deeper than that, shame twisted and writhed in the pit of his stomach. He folded his arms across his chest and pulled away from her touch.

"Crispin." She grasped his arm hard, and he turned to meet her intense gaze. "You are not your brother. I love you both equally, but you will never be Francis. You will never be your father. You are Crispin Saville, my son, the Prince of Whispers, gifted with a silver tongue and the power of persuasion. If anyone can turn this tragedy into a blessing, 'tis you. I have never been more proud of you as a son or as a king."

A knot formed in the pit of his stomach and slowly rose into his throat, choking him. "Even though I failed to save Francis from the fire? And attempted to pay someone to kill my own father?" He scoffed at the pain flashing in her blue eyes.

She released him and clutched the mug tightly between her hands. Tension filled the silence between them. Crispin raised his gaze to the heavens and closed his eyes. He was a fool to think she would forgive him for such a blatant betrayal.

"I am deeply wounded by this revelation," she spoke slowly, her tone measured and brimming with unchecked emotion. "But it does not surprise me." Their gazes locked once more and tears marred her loving face. "He was wrong to blame you for Francis's death. You were never going to be like Francis, and that was what he expected from you."

Crispin snorted as irritation filled him.

"We argued about it the night he banished you from the castle." She stared into the contents of her mug. "While I knew you needed a change, something to pull you from the hedonistic dredges in which you found yourself mired, I was not convinced stripping you of your funds and title would indeed garner the desired effect."

"Threatening to disinherit me completely made me reconsider my life, Mother." He could not keep the disdain from tarnishing his reply even though her confession made his heart twist inside his chest.

"I prayed you would find something to set you back in his good graces." She smiled. "Ruby was a gift from God, but it was not her alone who changed your heart or your actions. Those changes came from deep within you over time."

"My actions laid a course for Simon to set his plan into motion." Crispin rose to his feet and paced the small garden path. "Perhaps father had been correct in his decision to disinherit me and leave me to die alone and penniless. 'Tis what I deserve."

"Your father was wrong to use it as a weapon to force you to change and adapt, to try and mold you into a man you would never be." His mother set her tea aside and stood. She blocked the path, keeping him from pacing.

Crispin clenched his hands into fists as the agitation roiled inside him. He took several deep breaths but there were no words, only anger and frustration and regret.

"He was wrong, Crispin." Pride laced her words. "There is a passion burning inside of you that far outshines both your father and your brother." She grasped him by the shoulders. "You will do wonderful things for this country and our people. Both you and Ruby have endured so much and suffered such loss so early in your union, but I have seen growth and determination in you to overcome that which would have crippled your brother."

Straightening, Crispin stood taller at her declaration. Even through the lies and mistrust Simon attempted to use to manipulate and turn those he once trusted against him, his mother never abandoned hope. She believed in him, even when the whole kingdom thought him a wastrel and a deviant. Her faith bolstered his determination and courage. He would be the best king Meradin had ever seen.

"Taking the throne and binding yourself to Ruby simultaneously was a challenge you embraced with fervor." Her eyes sparkled in the winter afternoon light. "But make no mistake, you rose to the occasion, and it made you a better man as well as a more adept ruler. She balances you in ways no one else can. You need each other like the flowers need the sun to blossom and thrive."

"I nearly lost her." Crispin's mind replayed the moment he found her standing beside Simon after thinking she was dead. Fury engulfed him once more superseding the helpless pit of misery gaping in his chest. "I nearly lost Henry as well."

"'Tis true, but they survived because they are strong, like you." She cupped his face in her hands, warming his cool skin and infusing him with her vigor. "Marian has assured me Henry will recover completely with time and care." His mother regarded him carefully. "As for Ruby, well, I am sure you will have her with child again before the spring."

Crispin smiled at the thought of his wife round with his child. 'Twould be no hardship for him to take her to bed every night. He longed for the opportunity to bury himself inside Ruby, but she needed adequate rest before they engaged in pleasurable activities once again. It pained him not to be able to comfort his wife in every possible way. And fucking could be pleasurable while comforting both parties involved. A wicked grin split his lips at the thought.

"Perhaps you should focus your thoughts and attention on your royal duties rather than your husbandly duties first, my son." His mother released him and retrieved her mug from the bench.

"I am merely reflecting on the idea you placed in my mind, Mother." He opened the door for her and followed her into the warmer corridor. "You cannot blame a man for desiring his wife."

"I lay no blame at your feet for your natural urges, however, you must be gentle with her. Such a loss cannot be thrust aside carelessly." She glanced at him as they walked side by side toward the great hall.

Crispin understood and respected the delicacy of the grief Ruby bore. He himself bore it, however not to such an extreme extent. He had not carried the child nor felt the keen loss of its life growing within him. Ruby was strong and resilient, but she needed to heal her body and her heart before he plied her with physical affection.

"I fully intend to care for Ruby in a respectful manner, you need not worry on that count." Crispin pushed open the door into the great hall, causing the servants around the room to glance up at their arrival. They dipped low in respect and carried on with their duties.

His mother paused before they reached the head table and turned to face him. "Have you given thought to your punishment for Simon's treason?"

A plethora of possible means appeared in his mind, but Crispin could not voice such grotesque wickedness aloud to his mother. He merely gave a regal nod.

"I have, Mother, and you can rest assured I will mete out this justice and rid my conscience of Simon forever." He grinned. "But I will not soil your soul with such things."

"My soul is not as untarnished as you may think." She shook her head. "Perhaps 'tis better if I do not know what becomes of him. The less we dwell on his treason, the better we can heal."

"Perfectly said, Mother." Crispin bowed and left the great hall.

There was one thread left and he fully intended to unravel it before burning it to the ground. A vendetta awaited. But first, Crispin needed to deal with the only person left in this debacle that he did not trust.

Ruby's young maid passed him in the corridor.

"You there."

She stopped and bowed. "Your majesty, how may I serve?"

"Have Ivy come to my presence chamber, posthaste."

"At once, sire." The girl curtseyed and darted down the hall.

Crispin retreated to his presence chamber and poured some wine. While he would not deny his friend his love, he held no confidence in her loyalty to him or the people of Meradin. An understanding must be reached, but it would take time and action to ensure Ivy could be trusted within these walls.

The knock at the door pulled him from his thoughts. "Enter." He straightened to his full height.

Ivy entered, closing the door behind her. She wore a simple kirtle and gown, her chestnut hair hidden beneath a cap. "You summoned me, sire?"

"Aye. Come closer." He eyed her with suspicion. This woman created a whirlwind of chaos in her wake. Even though her actions allowed their escape, Crispin could not bring himself to trust anyone who was trained by the Guild.

"You told me you were sold to the Guild as a young child." Crispin leaned against his desk, his gaze focused on the woman before him.

"This is the truth, sire. I was purchased by the Guild and then trained to do their bidding." Ivy remained steadfast. Her voice strong and her words clear.

"They then sold you to the highest bidder as a trained assassin."

"I was trained in many things, sire." She cocked her head. "But for brevity's sake, the title of assassin fits adequately enough."

"And Simon purchased your contract, is this correct?"

"I knew not the identity of the man behind my purchase."

"But you have no doubts that man is Simon?"

"None, sire." Ivy straightened, her expression blank.

"Do you claim loyalty to him still?"

"Nay."

Crispin inclined his head, a feral smile curling his lips. "According to the code of the Guild, you are bound to him until such time as he releases you from your contract or he is dead."

Her eyes widen in surprise. "This is true."

"Then tell me, Ivy. How am I to place my trust in you? I cannot place my faith in you merely on the whimsical request of my lovelorn companion." His expression hardened. "Henry might be foolish enough to allow you possession of his heart and his protection. But I have much higher expectations than pretty promises and illusions of repentance."

"Your majesty, I…"

"Furthermore, your actions led to the death of my unborn child. A vile deed I cannot forgive." Crispin closed the distance between them, his fury barely tethered. "Can you deny your part in my queen's capture and the murder of our child?"

"I cannot, sire." All pretense dropped when Ivy lifted her gaze. "I vow, I knew nothing of Simon's intention to bring harm to the queen or kill her child. Had I known of his intentions, I would have intervened."

Crispin searched for some sign of duplicity or deception, and yet all he found were the haunting sounds of resignation in her tone.

"Do with me what you will, sire. I deserve punishment for my role in Simon's betrayal." Ivy's calm acceptance left Crispin stunned.

"Should I allow you to live out the rest of your days, what assurance do I have of your loyalty to the crown?" He circled her quiet form.

"I pledge myself completely."

Crispin's smile widened. "Shall we seal it in blood?"

"Blood, sire?"

"Aye, the blood of a traitor may wash away your sins." Crispin held her gaze for a long moment, unsure if his implication was understood. He could order her to kill Simon, but she must take the initiative to free herself from the Guild's bonds. "Cut away the last remaining ties to the Guild, and I will allow you a fresh start in my kingdom."

Ivy's expression brightened.

"Mark my words, should you fail in your task, should you betray me, I will string you up outside the gates and let the crows feast upon you as a warning to all traitors," Crispin growled.

"Aye, your majesty."

"Very well, you are dismissed." He called out as she reached the door. "Ivy."

She turned. "Sire?"

"This conversation does not leave my chamber, am I understood?"

"Of course." She nodded in acknowledgment and slipped quietly from the room.

Crispin poured a goblet of wine and sat before the fire. He

prayed his friend's misplaced love would not lead them into regret.

The next morning, Crispin woke to a commotion. Henry appeared, distraught, at his door bearing the news.

Simon was dead. Found in a pool of his own blood, his throat slit and a muted scream of horror on his scarred face.

Ivy earned her pardon at last.

Chapter Twenty-Five

The kingdom blossomed with hope when spring arrived in its full glory. Ruby spent the day in the gardens in the outer bailey with Marian and Ivy. While her mother refused to move to the castle permanently, she visited frequently, bringing gifts and visiting those along the way who required her services. The winter had been harsh for most in the kingdom, but Marian showed initiative to help those who needed her herbal knowledge and share it with those willing to learn.

Ivy had been quick to learn the trade. Ruby took pride in knowing her actions led to the salvation of a soul in need. While Crispin still eyed the woman with suspicion, Ruby trusted her implicitly.

Henry kept Ivy close. The two were united in a small ceremony on the coldest winter night in all her years. Ivy fell into a comfortable companionship with Ruby and Vivienne, but it was her bond with Marian which stunned Ruby the most. Another lost soul adopted by the wayward outlaw who sought refuge in the forests of Meradin so many years ago.

"I have finished planting the herbs in the far row." Ivy approached, wearing a dirt-smeared apron and a fitted cap hiding her dark curls from view. "Shall I fetch some water?"

"Have the young men fetch the water." Ruby wiped her soiled hands on her own apron and nodded with satisfaction at the sizable garden. Come the fall they would have a place to harvest many of their own herbs without having to rely on the monastery. A wave of sadness washed over her followed by nausea.

Ruby leaned against the fence and pressed her hand to her stomach to quell the sensation.

"Are you well?" Ivy appeared by her side in an instant.

"A momentary lapse. 'Tis gone now." She straightened and

stopped at the smile curving Ivy's lips. 'Twas so difficult to hide anything from her intuitive nature.

Ivy leaned close and whispered, "Have you told the king?"

So much for secrecy. Curse her body for betraying her. "I have not told a soul. I had hoped to wait a few months before revealing my condition."

"I am glad to see there was no time wasted in conceiving another heir." Ivy winked. "Come, let us return to the castle. You should tell him directly lest he discover it unwittingly."

"'Tis so soon. Should I not wait until the next moon to be certain?" Ruby resisted the urge to trail her hand over her abdomen as they walked toward the gate leading to the inner bailey. Something about this situation seemed vaguely familiar.

"I knew the moment I was with child and told Henry directly," Ivy murmured, but Ruby heard her clearly.

"Truly?" Joy filled her at the thought of them following this journey together. She took Ivy's hand in hers. "Why did you not tell me?"

Ivy bit her lip. "I did not want to hurt you by revealing my joy when you were still grieving your loss."

Ruby squeezed her hand at the thoughtful gesture. "My thanks. 'Tis not an easy thing to overcome. I doubt I ever shall forget the pain of such a devastating blow, but I have hope for what is to come. Surely time will ease the ache."

"Time does offer healing, but 'tis good to remember the lessons taught to us by our past." The innocuous statement from any other person would have been dismissed easily, but coming from Ivy, Ruby took it as profound growth of character.

Henry glanced up from the ring where he stood training the knights. He nodded at Ruby, but his gaze lingered on Ivy as they passed. Even from this distance, she saw the hunger in his determined expression as he watched his wife pass. She relished the knowledge Henry found someone who completed him so perfectly. He deserved some happiness after the torment he endured.

Inside the castle, Ivy helped her bathe and dress. Even though she was no longer her maid, Ivy tended her with a willingness to serve and loyalty no other servant could match. Their bond was unbreakable and everlasting. Sisters, not in blood, but in shared sacrifice and understanding.

Refreshed and renewed by her work and the aromatic bath, Ruby left her room determined to seek out Crispin. She wandered the corridors and paused outside the door to his presence chamber. With a solid knock, she waited.

His command to enter echoed through the wood. Ruby pressed her hand to her stomach and took a breath before opening the door.

Crispin's furrowed brow softened at the sight of her. "Ah, my queen, to what do I owe this delightful distraction?" His ravenous gaze shifted over the simple gown she wore. He pushed the chair back and patted his thigh in invitation.

Heat curled through her. Their time together intensified her desire for him.

"I did not wish to interrupt you while you worked." She crossed the room and sat on his lap. His arms snaked around her, holding her fast against him as he nuzzled against her neck.

"Your presence is always welcome." He pressed a kiss to her neck, and he grasped her breast in his palm, kneading until her nipple pebbled beneath his touch. "I missed your scent. It has been too long since I buried myself inside you."

Ruby chuckled before a moan erupted from her throat at his ministrations. "You—" she licked her lips "—It has only been a few hours."

"Aye." Crispin stroked his hands over her hips and drew up her skirt. "I woke at dawn and buried my cock deep in your cunt." He nipped at her shoulder while his fingertips brushed her bare thigh edging higher and higher until they brushed her aching core. "All night I dreamt of you. When I woke with you in my arms, I drove you to such pleasurable heights before sating us both. Tell me you do not crave more."

"Crispin—" Her breath caught in her throat as he stroked her slit finding the sensitive places with ease and teasing her until she grasped his wrist.

"I want you to coat my fingers with your arousal." His

demand made her body twitch. When he slid his fingers into her, she clung tighter as the pleasure overtook her. "Do you like when I tease you?" He moved slowly, thrusting with a measured pace.

Ruby bucked her hips against him. Her body ached for release. She nodded, biting her lip, unable to think only feel. Crispin overwhelmed her with his scent, his heat, his words.

"Please," she begged.

"So pretty when you stand on the precipice of release." He quickened his pace, stroking with masterful precision. "Beg for me, darling."

"Crispin, please, I need..." She gasped when he flicked her nub with his thumb. "I want..." The words twisted in her mind, jumbled by the haze of lust coursing through her. A cry built in her throat as her climax crested.

"Yes, my love." Crispin tipped her over the edge. He raked his teeth over her skin as she found her release.

She closed her eyes and collapsed against him when the burst of sensation ricocheted through her, drawing her higher into blissful awareness. When she finally opened her eyes, Crispin's wicked grin and sparkling eyes were the first things she saw.

"Quite a decadent distraction." Holding her gaze, he licked the arousal from his fingers. "Mmmm, so sweet. Perhaps I shall feast on you this evening. Bury my face between your thighs and lick your delicious cunt until you cry out in pleasure again and again."

Ruby's face heated at his words and actions, but she did not shy away from them. Instead, she embraced his wicked whispers, allowing them to burrow into her soul and feed her insatiable hunger for him.

"I do not believe your mother would appreciate us missing the lovely spring feast she has prepared." Ruby shifted to meet his gaze, noting the prominent press of his cock against her hip.

Crispin tucked a stray lock of hair behind her ear and her heart warmed at the tender gesture. "I would hate to disappoint my mother, but I would much rather spend my nights fucking my wife."

"The guests will assume you have decided to neglect your duties as king should you decide to remain hidden." She ran her fingers through his hair and gave a gentle tug.

"Fucking my wife is not neglecting my duties as king. I must ensure the continuation of the royal line." He hissed when she pulled a bit harder. His blue eyes darkened to the color of a midday storm.

"And if I told you there was no need to do so?" Ruby drew her lower lip between her teeth.

Crispin's eyes narrowed before the joyful smile transformed his face. "You are with child? So quickly?"

Ruby laughed. "You have made a valiant effort over the past few months. Nearly every night. Truth be told, I find your stamina quite endearing, but perhaps this will allow you to get some rest."

Crispin stood quickly and scooped Ruby into his arms. She squealed and clung to him as he carried her to the hidden door connecting his presence chamber to his bed chamber. He kicked the door shut with a shuddering determination.

By the time he placed her on the coverlet, her body wept for him. The climax he gave her moments before fell to the wayside like a distant memory. He claimed her mouth with his, promising something infinitely more pleasurable than his eager fingers coaxing pleasure from her willing body.

She trembled with anticipation as he plundered her lips. His teeth raked against the soft skin, drawing a moan from deep within her. When he ravished her thus, he unleashed a torrent of unexpected emotion.

Over the past few months, he seduced her in every way. With his words, his actions, his body. Every time different than the last. He grieved with her, but he also released the remaining hesitation keeping her from embracing her place beside him. He made her his queen in name, but after Simon, he allowed her to take her rightful place as queen in her own way.

He trailed kisses along her neck and down, tugging the gown aside to reveal her sensitive breasts. His gaze met hers as he suckled, pulling her nipples into tight peaks in his mouth. She buried her fingers in his hair and tugged. She wanted more. Needed more.

Breathless and panting, she arched her hips against his. He gathered her skirts in his fist and wrenched them up around her hips. With deft and practiced movements, he freed himself from his hose and drove his cock into her.

Ruby gasped and dug her fingernails into his shoulders.

"Saints, Ruby. Being inside you is nothing short of pure bliss." He groaned and thrust deeper. His eyes drifted closed for a brief moment before he locked his stormy gaze with hers. "'Tis the closest I shall come to heaven's gates. Being buried in your sweet quim, your cries sound like angel song to my wicked heart."

She wrapped her legs around him and held him close. "Such lovely words of seduction will earn you no reprieve. Perhaps I should put your silver tongue to better use."

"I relish the opportunity, my queen." He withdrew and drove deep. "But first, I shall fuck you until I milk every last drop of pleasure from your body leaving you sated. Then I will feast on you until your juices coat my face and you come on my tongue."

"My wicked king." Ruby pulled him close. Her kiss desperate and demanding as he moved inside her. There was nothing sweet and timid about their lovemaking.

Crispin's hips slammed into hers hard, pushing her deep into the linens covering the bed. He cursed the fabric of her gown as he shifted. Withdrawing long enough to remove the damned garment, Crispin ripped the fabric from her body and buried himself inside her.

The harsh fabric of his clothes chafed against her sensitized skin. Naked beneath him, Ruby reveled in his loss of control. She drove him to this point of pure lust-filled desperation. Her fingers tugged at her nipples with each stroke of his hips.

His eyes darkened at the sight. He took her wrists in his hands and pinned them to the bed.

"This night your pleasure belongs to me. I will take it at my leisure." He growled and kissed her. Then he laved the hard peaks with his tongue. The motion of his hips and his mouth falling in tandem, driving her pleasure to an unimaginable height. Her climax hovered out of reach. Crispin knew exactly how to push her to the edge but not allow her to fall into the pleasurable abyss.

"Have mercy," Ruby pleaded. Her body writhed beneath him. The abrasion of his clothes against her naked skin only intensified the sensations. As much as she longed for the feel of his bare skin against hers, she reveled in the contrast. He would take her as he wished. Mercy be damned.

"Trust me, sweeting. I will give you everything you deserve and beyond." His wicked grin filled her hazed vision.

Ruby bucked her hips against him when his rocked perfectly against her sensitive cleft. Her thoughts swirled into a massive cyclone spinning out of control in the midst of the sea. All her focus remained centered on Crispin and the spell he wove around her body.

Without warning, Crispin rolled onto his back, pulling her with him until she straddled his hips. Naked astride her fully clothed king, Ruby glared down at him.

"Take what you want, my queen." He licked his lips before drawing the lower between his teeth and moaning as she rocked her hips taking him deeper. "Use me as you wish. Take your pleasure. Deny me mine, if that is what you desire." The mischievous glint in his eyes lit a fire in her belly.

She braced her hands against his clothed chest. Her fingers slid against the velvet fabric with every movement. He thrust up to meet her, driving his body to brush the sensitive nub hidden between her folds.

Ruby tilted her head back and reveled in the power of her position. She rode him deep and hard. Their mingled moans echoed off the stone walls.

"Aye, sweeting. Louder. Let me hear your cries of pleasure." He encouraged her with his words while his hands on her hips kept her steady. Her movements grew more frenzied as she chased her release. "Perfection. Absolute perfection. How glorious you look riding my cock."

His filthy words increased the need building within her. She craved more and tipped her head back and the remaining restraint dissipated. Her cries ripped free from her chest.

Crispin's fingers pressed against the folds of her sex, sending her body into a spasm. The climax rushed through her like a raging river bursting from the mountains in the spring. Ruby fisted her hands in his doublet and collapsed against his chest.

The waves of pleasure washed over her making her tremble in his embrace. He stroked her shoulder and pressed a tender kiss to her forehead.

"Reminds me of that first night in the stables." He chuckled.

Ruby leaned back, searching his face. "Well, without the leather bindings."

"And if I remember correctly, you left me wanting." He grinned. "This time I am quite satisfied."

With a shake of her head, Ruby laughed. "Still insufferable."

He wrapped his hand around the back of her neck and drew her close for a lingering kiss. "And yet you still love me."

"Saints above help me, but I do. 'Tis an indisputable truth." Ruby melted against him.

They lay silent for a while until Ruby rose and gathered the ruined gown from the floor.

"What am I to wear to the feast now?" She held up the ruined garment with a pout.

Crispin propped himself on his side. His hungry gaze slid over her naked form, and she shivered at the bold lust in his eyes even after their ardent lovemaking.

"I told you before, I fully intend to keep you in this room until I have had my fill." He winked, but his tone brooked no argument.

"Your mother will be quite disappointed, Crispin." She propped her hand on her hip and sashayed closer, enjoying the way his jaw flexed at the sight before him. "Surely we can attend briefly and then seek our dessert elsewhere?"

"I cannot promise I will not pull you onto the table and

feast upon you in front of all our guests should the urge come upon me." Crispin arched his brow. She knew better than to ask whether he jested or not because he was scandalous enough to do as he pleased and the consequences be damned.

"If you can refrain from acting on your baser impulses, then I shall reward you once we are alone again." Ruby leaned down to press a kiss to his swollen lips.

He hooked his hand around her neck and delved his tongue between her lips. The invasion stole her breath and reignited the passion once more. Would she ever get enough of this man?

"What is my reward?" he murmured against her mouth.

"Me on my knees."

His left brow arched.

"Your cock in my mouth."

The right brow rose to compliment the left. A sinful grin stole across his lips. "Oh, what a sight that will be."

"You must control yourself during the feast," Ruby reminded him. "Do we have a bargain?"

"Seal it with a kiss."

She obliged him but drew away before he seduced her for another bout of bed sport. "Now, let us prepare for the feast before your mother sends Ivy to fetch us."

Crispin's countenance fell at the mention of Ivy. "Must you always ruin the moment?"

"'Tis not my fault you cannot overcome your distrust of Henry's bride." Ruby backed away and retrieved a gown from Crispin's wardrobe.

"She is dangerous." Crispin rose from the bed and tucked his cock out of sight.

"Aye, but she has redeemed herself and pledged loyalty to the king and queen of Meradin." She wagged a finger at him. "You pardoned her on your own conscience, remember."

Crispin ran his hand through his hair. "I could not execute the love of my closest friend. I nearly lost Henry once, such an act would surely sever our bond. He would never forgive me for such a blow."

"Do you still distrust her so?" Ruby asked, curious as to his position considering the contradiction of his pardon. She pulled the gown over her head and struggled with the laces.

"'Tis in my nature to be distrusting." Crispin nudged her hands aside and laced the gown himself.

"Do you trust me?" Ruby glanced at him, studying his stern profile.

"Aye." His blue eyes met hers. "With my life." Sadness marred his brow. "I cannot live without you, Ruby. You are my salvation and for that, I am eternally bound in gratitude. But in all truth, I know no one who completes me as you do. I trust no one as I trust you."

With tears in her eyes, Ruby turned and wrapped her arms around him. "Oh Crispin, what a pair we are. Enemies bound by fate turned lovers by destiny." She kissed him and savored the feel of his strength and stability.

"I love you, Ruby." Crispin stroked her cheek with his thumb.

"And I love you, Crispin, my Prince of Whispers."

"King," Crispin corrected her. "King of Whispers."

Ruby laughed. "So long as those wicked whispers are only for me."

"Always, my love. Always." He kissed her again. All thoughts of the feast forgotten.

The End

Hello again,

Thank you so much for reading this book. If you enjoyed it, even a little, would you do me a huge favor? Please take a few minutes and write a review, and if you know someone who would enjoy this book, send them a little note and tell them about it.

If you're intimidated by writing a review, here's a blog post I wrote a few years ago to help readers formulate a helpful review: **https://kirstensblacketer.com/2018/01/11/how-to-write-a-helpful-review/**

An honest review is like a love letter to the author. It helps us grow and lets us know our hard work is appreciated. Though it may seem simple and insignificant, it means the world to hear your thoughts. Thank you for taking the time to show your love.

Also, if you'd like to be the first to know when I have a new release or get some sneak peeks into my current WIPs, then sign up for my monthly newsletter. When you subscribe, you'll get a free steamy historical short story. You can only get it as a loyal subscriber to my newsletter. I'll be offering other special short stories and giveaways as well. You won't want to miss it. You can find the sign up form on my website:

https://kirstensblacketer.com

Thank you again for your love and support! I look forward to chatting with you soon.

Sincerely,

Jen Bradlee/Kirsten S. Blacketer

ABOUT THE AUTHOR

Jen Bradlee is the alter ego of author Kirsten S. Blacketer.

Jen Bradlee can get away with murder, metaphorically speaking of course. She enjoys people watching, belly dancing, and taking walks in the rain. Give her a man who isn't afraid to get his hands dirty and plays hard. The ones with rough edges and a little scruff are the best. Comes with a warning label. "Too hot to handle."

Inspired by Tom Hiddleston and Benedict Cumberbatch, she creates characters who have multiple facets to them. The gentleman in the streets but with a wild, dangerous side behind closed doors. She loves villains and anti-heroes, bad boys and irredeemable men. We all have a dark side. Sometimes it must be freed.

http://kirstensblacketer.com/jen-bradlee